Footprints in History

Footprints in History

J. M. Goodison

History Buff Press

Montana

This story is based on actual people and events. However, my rendition of the characters, incidents, situations, and circumstances have been fictionalized. Any errors are mine alone.

Cover design by Janice McCaffrey and Bonnie Smith

Landscape photo by Logan Lybbert

History Buff Press

Montana

Dedication

To all the Fitchetts before me who have left their footprints in history to give me the freedoms and privileges I enjoy. And a special thanks to Dennis Cole, the cousin, who first introduced me to James Fitchett.

The work you are about to read is a fictionalized biography of my seventh great grandfather, James Fitchett as he and his neighbors left their footprints in the history of Perth Amboy, New Jersey and Staten Island, New York.

J. M. Goodison

Storm clouds portend disaster

Blue skies raise hopes for good fortune

Anonymous

The Apprentice

October 1677

"James, since we lost your father, I've tried to support us. I've sold everything I could." His mother, her expression uneasy, sat on the settee across from him. She scanned the small, cozy sitting room, smoothed her apron across her lap, and then looked back into his eyes. After a deep breath she continued, "I've accepted Mr. Bell's marriage proposal. I'll live with him above his shop."

"You're leaving me?" His eyes pleaded against her abandonment.

"No, James, I'm not leaving you. We'll see one another often. You're growing up. You need to be on your own."

Even though he sat in his favorite chair—his favorite because he remembered helping cook stuff the cushions after several of her delicious goose roasts—comfort eluded him. He squirmed as he listened.

"I've protected you from becoming a fisherman like your father. I couldn't bear it if you were to drown, too. But now you must support yourself and you have no trade. Blacksmith Ramsay needs an apprentice. Mr. Bell spoke with him, and they've agreed, you'll fill the position. You'll live with the Ramsays. This house has sold."

Flopping his long, thin arms at his sides, he groaned, "Oh, Ma, I can't be a blacksmith I don't have the muscle."

"You'll become stronger as you learn the trade."

His whining went on, "And the smithy is always filthy."

1

Annoyance mingled with his mother's words. "James, you'll be seventeen in two weeks. You're not a child. It's true I've never given you responsibilities. I let you spend time with your friends playing that tin whistle your father gave you. But now you must be a man and support yourself. And someday, God willing, a family."

James stood in defiance to his mother's plans. Fists tight he spewed out alternatives. "I can learn another trade. Or I could help Mr. Bell. I know my ciphers. I wouldn't make mistakes with accounts. I can read and write. I could stock the shelves."

"You'll be Blacksmith Ramsay's apprentice for the next seven years. And we won't discuss this again." His mother stood and walked away from him into the kitchen.

A sour taste settled on his dry tongue. Fighting tears, he whispered, "Mother, if I fail, I'll be homeless and hungry." James looked down at his feet. Like a reprimanded dog, tail between its legs, he slunk up the stairs to his bedroom.

He sat on the edge of his narrow bed and stared out the window without seeing the gray sky or the rain dancing on his mother's rose garden. Shaking his head, he used both hands to push his fine, fair hair off his forehead then reached for his tin whistle. As he blew a melancholy ballad, he realized the futility of his argument and began wondering how life might be as a master blacksmith.

James created a vision of himself forging lumps of iron into useful tools, a respected member of society with many friends. He imagined groups of young ladies watching him work, giggling about his muscular arms and chest. Unbidden, a smile found its way to his smooth face. The tension in his forehead relaxed. He mumbled aloud, "Maybe it won't be so bad."

Singing his favorite ditty, he changed into his dancing attire for the evening's social.

James hoped Jean would be there. He wanted to tell her about his apprenticeship before she heard about it from someone else. He wanted her to be proud of him. They'd been friends since childhood. Though lately he'd found his thoughts about her taking on a more grown-up, serious feel. A sympathetic friend, she always lifted his spirits with her smile. But he hoped, in time, she would see him as a man who could take care of her. Some people might think a blacksmith wasn't as good as they were, but he was sure Jean was different. She'd help him face his inevitable future. A future he never imagined for himself.

■■■

Later that night as James pulled the blankets up to his chin, he reflected on his evening. He smiled as he remembered the light-hearted fun he enjoyed with his friends, especially Jean. For an instant she had looked shocked when he told her about his apprenticeship, but she had managed to treat him as she always had. He smiled, *she's a true lady and a true friend.*

But all too soon his thoughts reverted to the conversation with his mother. Self-pity returned oozing into his heart. *I like my life. Why must Mother push me out? I'm not ready.*

He wrapped his arms around his stomach and curled up, knees almost to his chin. Unable to conquer his unrelenting dread, he stared into the darkness.

■■■

That inevitable day in late October James' mother tried to engage him in frivolous conversation, but he remained quiet. His somber mood lingered as he packed his clothes, tin whistle, and spyglass into his father's sea bag. He remembered using the spyglass to watch for his father's ship returning to the Montrose Harbor. He wished his father were there. His life wouldn't be changing if his father were still alive.

Disoriented, he walked away from the two-story stone house his grandfather's successful merchant business had built. His lips set in a grim line, James dawdled along High Street watching people going in or out of merchants' shops. He passed the church's steps and looked up at its tall steeple.

Montrose Scotland 1678   Sketch by Captain Slezer

Leaving the city behind, he approached the docks and walked Wharf Street. Watching seaman disembark their ships and greet waiting loved ones caused a familiar ache in his heart. He missed his father and their reunions. After leaving America Street behind, he kicked at the ground. Head hanging, he plodded along the worn path east, toward the beach where his parents had met, to Blacksmith Ramsay's cabin. A light wind ruffled his hair. He heard the waves hitting the sand and the seagulls cawing to one another.

Answering James' timid knock, the muscular smithy greeted him with a smile and firm handshake then pulled him in the cabin door. "Welcome to your future, James."

James looked around. The place was small. It was obvious that cooking, dining, and sitting all took place in this one room. There was a closed door in the rear wall. He assumed it led to Ramsey's bed chamber. He shuffled his feet. *Where will I fit?*

Mrs. Ramsay turned from the table where she'd been peeling potatoes. Her loud greeting surprised James. Her stature, elfin-like compared to her burly husband, belied her boisterous greeting, "Come, James, I'll show you the loft where you'll sleep. You can put your duffle up there. I think there're plenty of quilts, but if you need more, let me know. Breakfast is served at six and the evening meal at eight. I'll bring the mid-day meal to the forge. Mr. Ramsay doesn't like to stop work long to eat." She didn't seem to take a breath between words. "Monday is laundry-day. Give me your dirties before breakfast. I get an early start."

The Ramsays had no children. James had heard townsfolk say Mrs. Ramsay liked to 'mother' the apprentices and always made sure 'her boys' had enough to eat. Mrs. Ramsay put her hands on her narrow hips, "What foods do you like? I know everyone has their favorites."

■■■

As soon as he finished eating, not dinner as he had with his family, but what Mrs. Ramsay called supper, James went to the cabin's loft. Not to sleep. To be alone. He lit the single candle and investigated the shadows. Flavors of beef stew clung to his tongue even though he hadn't eaten much. He thought about what tomorrow would bring and his stomach churned. The vision of him as a muscular, successful blacksmith evaded him.

Aware of his shaky hands, he unpacked his duffel, placing his change of clothes on the shelves provided, and undressed. Lying on the straw filled ticking, he stared at the shadows dancing in the rafters. He heard cattle lowing and chickens clucking, strange noises to him. This close to the sea, the gulls' piercing screeches assaulted his ears. James had grown-up in the city of Montrose. He missed hearing people's voices and horses' hooves clomping on the cobblestones. He didn't miss the grunting pigs eating the household garbage and waste from the streets below his bedroom window.

It seemed to James he'd fallen asleep a few short minutes before he heard the Ramseys stirring, much earlier than his usual rising time. Before day dawned James struggled to his feet and made haste to dress in the rough trousers and shirt his mother had purchased for him. He was used to finer clothing.

A plain but hearty breakfast sat on the round wood table before an empty chair. His mouth watered as he spotted the creamy looking porridge, a thick slice of Mrs. Ramsay's home-baked bread with butter, and a cup of strong tea. He sat and ate as much as he dared, not sure his stomach would keep it.

As the sun broke over the eastern horizon, Mr. Ramsay led James from his cabin about twenty-feet along the shoreline to the forge, all the time making small-talk. James guessed it was his master's way to distract nervous apprentices. But the plan failed. Terror rendered James speechless.

Ramsey opened two barn doors as wide as they'd go. He stepped in and took a dark-brown leather garment from a nail in the wall.

"Here's your apron." The Master Blacksmith tossed a filthy-looking garment to James.

Catching it between his right thumb and index finger James looked at it like it might carry a contagious disease. "Ugh." He gasped. *Did I say that out loud?* The foul thing made breakfast churn in his stomach. He swallowed hard.

The Master held his apron so James could see its top, then placed the round strap over his head hanging the apron from his neck. He placed the bulk of the heavy leather across his body, wrapped the straps around his middle and back again tying them into a tight square-knot.

James wrinkled his nose, and clinching his jaw, wrestled with the apron. It got twisted every which way. But task accomplished, apron right-side-up and straps tied, he nodded.

The barn-like shop looked more akin to a dark, grimy cave to James. He shivered as he stepped inside. As his eyes adjusted, the dim light presented sundry tools to his view. He cocked his head to the side as he surveyed them. He saw peculiar hammers, files, chisels, pliers, wrenches, and an unimaginable number of tongs in various shapes and sizes. A soft whistle escaped his pursed lips. Ramsay smiled at his student's response then pointed to and named every implement insisting each be returned to its precise spot straight away after use.

James scanned the rest of the shop. A work bench took up the back wall. A side wall was covered with sagging shelves laden with lumps of iron, nails, horseshoes, shovels, and many items James couldn't begin to identify.

Smith Ramsay stopped at the bellows, "I'll show you how to use the bellows without the fire lit. It's safer that way." He explained as he went through the motions, "Stand straight, shoulders back, legs spread to keep your equilibrium. Your left foot flat, right foot's heel firm on the ground, its ball and toes on the foot-pedal ready to tap.

"The bellows manages the heat. When you pump the foot-pedal air is pushed under the fire, stoking it, building the fire. For less heat, stop pumping." Stepping aside, he motioned James to have a go.

James struggled in his attempts to copy the stance. He floundered, stumbling toward either the fire-pit or slack-tub full of dank water. Not wanting to fall into hot coals, he determined to practice when no fire burned.

"Stand opposite the work area facing me and watch everything I do."

The boy nodded and took his place.

"First thing every morning you'll light the forge fire," the blacksmith said lifting charcoal and kindling from nearby bins. He arranged them in the deep brick-bowl then rubbed flint on steel to spark flames to life.

Smoke replaced air. James coughed. His eyes stung. He used his shirt sleeve to wipe away uncontrollable tears.

Ramsay pumped the bellow's pedal encouraging the burn. Once it took hold, the smoke cleared. He continued, "Here fire's the center of life. Its temperature must be high to soften the iron enough so it can be re-shaped with hammers. But if the iron is too hot it won't hold its new shape. It's essential to use the right temperature for each job."

He laughed, "My mother must've had a premonition when she named me Aiden. In Gaelic it means fire. It's certain this indispensable fire is the center of my life. It supports my wife, me, and the entire community."

James thought it would take a long time for the fire to reach a high temperature, but it wasn't more than a few minutes before Smith Ramsay selected a tong, two long hinged arms with wide, flat ends. He manipulated the tool clasping a lump of iron from the pile on the floor, shoved the iron into the fire, and pumped the bellows foot-pedal increasing the heat.

A burst of scorching air hit James' face. He jumped out of its way. The reek of burning hair filled his nostrils. Instinct moved his hands to his face and hair checking for cinders. Shaking his head from side-to-side he quick-stepped back to his assigned position.

As soon as the metal turned red-hot Ramsay swung it out of the fire, positioning the hot mass on the anvil's flat surface. With the tongs in one hand and a hammer in the other he repeated striking the hot piece of iron.

Open-mouthed and wide-eyed James stared as the iron gave way. He leaned in for a closer look just as Ramsay plunged the fiery iron into the slack tub's cold water creating a burst of scorching steam. James sprang backward darting from the searing-mist. His body shook. He took a deep breath and while returning to his designated spot used both hands to push his damp hair off his sweaty forehead.

The blacksmith kept his eyes on the slack-tub, avoiding James' eyes, and continued the lesson. "Getting the molten material cold right away tempers it. Makes it hold its new shape." He looked at the piece of iron then at his young apprentice.

"You know, James, this process reminds me of life. Men are like the iron. Trials and temptations are God's fire." As he spoke, he placed the iron back into the coals and pumped the bellows. "If we soften our hearts when we're in His fervor, like the iron softens in this pit, His divinity will reshape us. Then He'll use mercy, His water, to temper us.

"God's grace builds valiant men who care for their families and live to the glory of God. The kind of men the Lord wants us to be."

Knees shaking, James silently begged, Please, God, don't ever throw me in Your fire.

"Cat got your tongue? You haven't said a word since breakfast."

James pushed aside his prayer. "Huh? Ah. . . No."

Instructions resumed as Ramsay's tongs held the hot iron on the anvil again. He pointed to an oversized hammer near the anvil, "As apprentice you're the striker."

With sudden understanding James scurried to the hammer. Having no idea its weight, he failed hefting it one-handed. His face took on a reddish flush. Gritting his teeth, he wrapped both hands around the wooden handle and lifted it over his shoulder. His arms shook. He teetered from the weight. He swung aiming for the hot iron on the anvil.

"Ow." Cramps gripped his back, shoulders, and upper arms. The hammer flew past the anvil throwing James off-kilter and onto the floor with a thud.

Stifling laughter, Ramsay, set the iron and tongs on the floor at his feet.

Bent forward, James grappled for stability. He rubbed his stinging palms together and grimaced as he straightened his back. Then, without intent, shoulders slumping, head hanging he stared at his feet.

"You need to be patient, James." Kindness intertwined with his master's words. James raised his head and looked into empathetic eyes.

"Changing a lump of iron into a useful object takes experience. It'll take time to build your confidence, but you will get there. You'll learn step-by-step. No rush. You have seven years. Most important, learn precision." The smith walked to a shelf and picked up a horseshoe.

Turning, he pointed the U-shape at James, "This horseshoe looks inconsequential, but horses need to maneuver on different surfaces without hurting their hooves. Farmers need steady-footed plow-horses. Horseshoes keep horses and people safe.

"Tools you forge will give people the ability to build houses and grow crops. Someday, James, families will rely on you. You'll see. You'll change the world around you."

Staring trance-like James murmured, "Me? Change the world?"

April 1678

After six months and the physical labor, James' muscles firmed and so did his self-confidence. A small glimmer of hope ever so slowly entered his heart. Someday, he thought, I might just succeed as a blacksmith after all.

However, there were two negative aspects of the work. First, he had little time for socializing, to be specific, little time to socialize with young women. Second, his standing in the community was lower than it had been.

At the beginning of his apprenticeship, James thought his friends were staying away to give him room to learn. But when he called at their home's servants told him either they were out or indisposed. After several attempts, he gave up, realizing they'd never be his friends again.

He missed her friendship and bright smile but even Jean stopped speaking to him. He'd heard she was engaged to a well-bred man from a prominent family.

Watching his friends move on with their lives, James understood the correctness of his mother's assertions. He had been a privileged, protected boy living in the shadow of his grandfather. Thrust out of his inherent social order, he'd become a mere laborer. No matter how hard he worked he'd never be more, an ordinary man serving higher regarded men.

Perturbed, James often muttered to himself, "It's not fair, it's just not fair."

...

Most Sunday afternoons James walked the beach or sat on the dock playing his tin whistle and listening to the seamen's' tall tales. But every Sunday evening he washed up and joined his mother and Mr. Bell for their evening meal. His mother seemed content. Mr. Bell treated James with courtesy, a guest in the man's home, he'd never be more.

Mr. Bell was a quiet man set in his habits. He'd been a widower for six months and missed the comforts his wife had afforded him. He wanted a woman's touch in his little apartment above the shop. He thought Euphemia Fitchett would bring that into his life. He wasn't disappointed, but she was different than he had imagined, more aloof. He hoped she was at least content as his helpmate.

For Euphemia's part she had never known life without a staff of servants to care for her home. Living with Mr. Bell she had but one woman who cleaned, took care of laundry, shopped, and prepared supper each day. Euphemia accepted her role in preparing breakfast and a mid-day meal but bulked at picking up after her new husband. Why he absent-mindedly left his dirty stockings on the floor she couldn't tell. Had his wife allowed that or was he testing her now in her new role. He had seemed like a thoughtful gentleman when he was courting her.

She missed Alex and if she were honest with herself, she missed the time to herself when he had been out to sea. She didn't mind helping in Bell's shop, but there was no space for her to be alone in her thoughts. And only in her dreams could she experience the deep desires she had felt for her one true love. Mr. Bell was considerate, but clumsy when it came to intimate relations.

She often stopped to count her blessings and openly show her gratitude to her husband. She couldn't picture in her mind where she would be without him. She had come to the end of her resources and had no way of supporting herself and her son. She hoped James would one day forgive her for forcing him into the apprenticeship with Blacksmith Ramsey.

One Friday night as Ramsay and James were cleaning up for supper, Ramsay asked, "James, why don't you go to the Black Horse Tavern tomorrow? Apprentices and servants your age go there. You could make some friends."

"I've never been inside a tavern. I'll think about it."

And think about it he did, most of the night. Tossing, turning, and fretting about what he might find at the Black Horse. The next day after supper James pulled his courage together and headed for George Street.

Hoping Mr. Ramsay was right, James entered the tavern. Its dark walls and painted windows lent a mysterious atmosphere to the place. He walked to the bar with as much swagger as he could muster, slapped a coin on the bar, and hollered, "A pint of ale."

Without showing any interest in his new customer, the old man behind the bar filled a mug from a barrel, set it in front of James, and picked up the coin.

James lifted the mug and took a sip. Not used to drinking hard brew, his grimace showed the bitterness of the hops. He stood straight, took a deep breath, and emptied the mug. Slapping another coin on the bar he thought he shouted, "Bar keep, another pint." But when the man ignored his order, James realized his words had come out as a mere squeak. He forced his voice louder to be heard over the noise of the crowd.

Conversation came from down the bar, "Isn't that James Fitchett? Why's he in this tavern?"

"His father drowned, and his mother remarried. He's Ramsay's apprentice. No more highbrow parties for him."

Showing no interest in what he heard, James drained the second mug. The room began to swirl, he grabbed the edge of the bar and hung on tight. A tidal wave of ale rocked his stomach. A hand over his mouth he rushed toward the door. A few steps away from the cool evening air a local ruffian bumped him. "Watch where yer goin'." He shoved James hard.

Baffled, James staggered forward, but didn't get to the door before another push sent him to the floor. Looking up James saw a man leaning over him with a mean smirk on his face. "Come on, get up. I'll have another swipe at ya."

James couldn't even pretend to protect himself. Everyone watched as the thug lifted James up by his collar and threw him out the door into the dust.

The following morning James winced in pain from even a small movement. He'd only vague memories of how he'd come to this. *What did I do wrong?* Ashamed, he didn't mention it to Mr. Ramsay.

However, not deterred from his goal to fit in with the working class, the following Saturday evening he returned to the same tavern. This time, his swagger not as strong. He could feel his knees shake as he tried to appear fearless. James ordered a pint and began sipping the foamy, bronze liquid when a well-built man with blonde hair cut short approached him. The stranger was taller than James' own five-foot-ten-inches. Expecting a fist to his chin, James ducked his head toward the bar then heard, "I'm Will Brodie, one of Mudie's stablemen. You new in town? Haven't seen you in here before."

Relieved James gave his name and occupation then offered his hand. He expected Will's handshake to be firm and it didn't disappoint. James noticed most the women in the tavern turned their eyes toward Will, but it seemed the man ignored them.

Will and James found they had a great deal in common and both enjoyed a good joke. As they parted company Will said, "See you at smithies next week. A Mudie horse needs a shoe replaced."

The two young men became good mates, neither one often seen without the other. From then on whenever James went to the Black

Horse, he ordered cider and drank slow. He didn't want to repeat his first encounter with ale.

Will introduced him to other servants and James found his niche in their community. James became accustomed to the tavern's sounds, women giggling, men cursing, telling outrageous stories, arguing, and occasional fist-a-cuffing.

The Tavern's aromas were comforting, stale ale, tobacco smoke, ham roasting on the spit, and bread baking in the oven. James came to enjoy cool breezes from open windows during summer and smoky warmth from its hearth in winter.

Years passed, in some ways one as the same as the other. James grew stronger physically and learned to put his full energies into his work. He became grateful to Mr. Ramsey for the patience he showed over the years in teaching the blacksmith trade. James laughed to himself as he remembered his daydream of himself working as a capable smithy with girls giggling as they watched his muscles flex. It hadn't been exactly like that, but he had had his fair share of willing servant girls to flirt with.

There had been one painful event in sixteen-eighty-two. His mother passed away. Thankfully, it had been sudden. She hadn't suffered. Since then instead of vising Mr. Bell on Sundays James walked to the cemetery. At her grave he would tell her about the week's events, his worries, and sometimes he'd offer a funny story he'd heard. In the summer he left roses on her grave. She had missed her rose garden after she'd moved in with Mr. Bell. And James played her favorite tune on his tin whistle before he left to meet Will.

America, Land of Opportunity

June 1684

One pleasant June day as Will and James walked along High Street, they heard a commotion. A crowd had gathered at the marketplace. The two friends lengthened their strides to see why. A person who could read the King's English shouted the words from the printed page nailed to the public notice wall.

"Its advertising land for sale and opportunities for tradesmen in Eastern New Jersey, in the Americas," he shouted. "Anyone who wants to make the voyage but doesn't have the money can sign up as an indentured servant. The cost of their transport will be paid, and they will be well-maintained in meat and clothing for four years."

A different voice informed the group. "Servants must work four years for the gentleman who pays their voyage."

Then another man's treble singsong mocked the words on the poster, "After four years the servants will be free and can live like gentlemen given land of their own."

Everyone laughed at that empty promise and gossiped as they dispersed.

James walked closer to read the broadsheet for himself. It listed ships leaving the city's port that autumn and directed interested parties to apply at the office of Doctor John Gordon in Montrose. Will and James both shrugged their shoulders and walked on. James was in the last months of his apprenticeship, but neither he nor Will had thoughts about leaving.

Knowing James had been friends with Jean Mudie, Will shared whatever gossip he heard about the family including Jean's marriage five-years ago and about the two children she and her husband were raising. A few days after they'd seen the broad sheet, Will told James, "Mr. Mudie and his wife have been heard arguing about Mudie's plan to go to America." Laughing, he added, "The servants are taking bets the wife will win and Mudie will stay. At least we're hoping. None of us want to lose our positions."

...

That September gossips spread the news. In the coming November, Mr. Mudie and four of his children would sail to America. The servants spared no details in their telling of the angry discussions between husband and wife about these latest arrangements for the family.

Walking with James to the Black Horse Tavern Will recounted the servants' stories. "Mrs. Mudie told her husband he would be cruel to force her and the children to leave their civilized country to live with savages in the Americas. She said she'd heard stories about colonist being tortured and murdered by the Indians and she feared for their lives." Will grinned as he said, "She even reminded him that he is nearly fifty-years-old and has no business gallivanting around the world."

As James listened, he remembered Jean's father, a short, plump man who dressed in fashionable suits wanting to impress his neighbors with his success.

Will went on, "The housemaids worried for Mudie's health. They said Mr. Mudie appeared exhausted, no longer enjoyed his usual hearty appetite, and at times he looked near insane."

18

Ambling up Baltic Street to George Street toward the tavern, Will related more of the story, "Monday last week, after the children left the dinner table, Mrs. Mudie told her husband she thought he should go to America. One of the servants told me Mudie's face lit up with excitement as he replied, 'Isobel, you've made me the happiest man in Scotland. I'll make arrangements for our voyage first thing in the morning.' But before he could even blink, she said, 'No, David, I won't go. I want you to go and find out for yourself—your wild plans will fail. It will end like your great drainage idea. In a disaster. I'll be here waiting when you return.'"

Mrs. Mudie's insults shocked James, but Will said, "She has a sharp tongue with her family. You know Jessie, the maid with the dark curly hair?"

James smiled, "Yes, I know Jessie. Why?"

Will answered James after they had walked past a carriage of laughing gentlemen stopped at the side of the street. "She told me that Mudie stood up for himself reminding his wife that the Dronner's Dyke Company back in seventy-six would've been a lucrative investment with the contract to drain the Montrose marsh if Witch Meggie Cowie hadn't caused the hurricane that destroyed the dyke. Then Mudie chided, reminding her that all his other investments had been profitable. He said, 'You certainly enjoy spending the money my malt cobel brings. I'm convinced I'll be successful in America, and I want you by my side.' But Mrs. Mudie said, 'No, David, I won't leave my home.' Then she stormed out of the room.

"Matthew, the gardener, saw Mudie leave his house, his head hanging. But when I saw him a couple hours later, he stood tall and looked resolute. I heard that later at dinner he informed his children of his plans. That he'd go to America alone, but that he'd be back in two years.

"According to Jessie, chatter turned to dead silence. The children all looked perplexed. 'It's all right.' Mrs. Mudie smiled and said, 'The mill and shop will support us while your father is off on his adventure.'

"But then Junior and James, remember they're twenty and twenty-one years of age, surprised their parents both shouting that they wanted to go. They pled, 'We can help you, Father. We'd be more help there than we are here. Your hired men can run the mill and the shop.'

"Mudie tried to contain his look of pleasure in his sons' enthusiasm as he muttered, 'I don't know, lads, your mother needs you here.'

"Both lads' shoulders slumped and neither spoke. Then Mrs. Mudie declared, 'Hogwash, I'll do fine without the two of you. John is six years old. He can be the man of the house while the three of you are gone.'

'Father, what's your decision?' Junior asked in almost a whisper.

"Mr. Mudie put a hand on each of the boys' shoulders, 'I'll be proud to have you with me.' The boys punched each other's upper arms. That's what I know and I'm sure the servants will have more details for us. Come on."

Will and James entered the tavern to find Mudie's servants excited to share the latest. Once everyone had a drink, Agnes, the ginger-haired upstairs maid, entertained them with what she'd heard, "I stopped in the hall outside-ah Issy and Margaret's bedroom. I 'erd em talk 'bout ther brothers' adventure. The more they talked 'bout it the more excited they sounded."

The eavesdropping maid carried on her commentary "I 'erd Issy coo, 'true, woman's place is in the home . . .' I imagined a bright twinkle in Issy's eyes as she continued, 'but don't father and the boys need a woman? Or better yet two women to keep their house and cook for them?'

"Margaret sounded delighted on account-ah Issy thought they could both help their men folk in the new land. Springs squeaked like they was a-jumpin' on the bed and I 'erd Margaret promise her sister, 'Tomorrow I'll convince father to take us, too.'"

For James' information Agnes added, "The whole town knows those two lassies are smart and gettin' ready to marry. They 'ave suitors, they do. But here they are a wantin' ta go to America."

Will told James, "Margaret is her father's favorite daughter, everyone knows and accepts that fact. None of the servants doubted the outcome."

Before James could think through all the new information, Matthew, the gardener, a quiet man with weathered skin, raised his pint of ale signifying he had part of the story to tell. He described the events he saw in the garden the following day, "Marget and Isbel had been in the garden playing hide and seek with their younger sisters when they saw Mudie leaving the house. Marget ran ta catch her Fa afore he left ta make arrangements fer the voyage. The lass give 'em 'er shy smile, 'Father, I'll miss you too much if you leave us. I'll be so sad.'"

At this Agnes popped up and pantomimed the rest of the interchange pretending to be Margaret. Will took up the part of the father patting Agnes on the head as Matthew continued.

"Er fa patted 'er head. 'Margaret, you'll be fine. We can write. Ships carry mail across the Atlantic often these days.'"

Continuing, Agnes looked at the floor, then made eye contact with Will, and again looked down. Moving side-to-side she purred, "'But, Father, who will cook and keep house for you?'"

Will answered in a deeper voice than his usual, "'I'm sure we'll find a woman to hire.'"

The charade went on between Agnes and Will.

"'But Father, Issy and I know how to cook and keep house. We ride and aren't afraid to live in rough circumstances. Couldn't we go with you? Please?'"

"'How could you even imagine doing such a thing? You and Issy are young ladies. You should be seeing young men and looking forward to keeping your own houses.'

"'Oh, Father,'" Agnes, mimicking Margaret, sighed with exasperation. "'Why can't girls have adventure? Why do the boys get all the opportunities and we girls get stuck at home?'"

Matthew finished, "Tha' ol' man went back in tha house a-shakin' his head."

Jessie, the downstairs maid with the frizzy, dark hair she couldn't keep under her cap, picked up the story. "I began polishing the furniture near the library door when I heard Mudie come in. Mrs. Mudie sat at her desk writing notes. Attempting to imitate her Master, Jessie bellowed, "'Isobel! Margaret and Issy want to go to the colonies with the boys and me. How did they get such an idea?'"

Jessie answered herself in falsetto voice, "'Well, David, I don't know. I'll speak with them.'"

Returning to her normal pitch Jessie said, "Mrs. Mudie left the library and went out to the garden."

Matthew picked up the garden scene. "Workin' close by I 'erd and saw wha' happen'd next. Mrs. Mudie demanded, 'What are you girls thinking, asking your father to take you with him to that uncivilized land?'"

Again, Agnes jumped in as Margaret, straightening her back and standing upright Agnes looked Jessie in the eye, as Margaret had looked at her mother. "'Mother, we know how to cook and keep house, we shoot, ride, and enjoy being in the country. We want an adventure before we settle down as wives and mothers living predictable lives. We can take care of father and our brothers. We can give them a more refined environment than they would provide for themselves or with a hired woman.' The girl hardly took a breath, 'We've decided to go. If you stop us, I'll never forgive you.'"

Jessie stared looking stunned as Mrs. Mudie had. Then Jessie stomped her feet showing how the woman had returned to the house.

As a side-note, Will added, "Matthew, also stunned, knows, as all the servants know, none of her children had ever spoken to her with such determination or rebellion."

Jessie returned to her narration, "Mudie remained in the library waiting. I kept working near the doorway. Mrs. Mudie's face looked stern as she walked in and said, 'Take them. I think the experience will do those girls more good than staying here with me.' Looking lighthearted for the first time in weeks, Mudie walked out of the library, beaming as he headed out to the garden."

Matthew laughed out loud as he declared, "The whole town coulda 'erd Mudie shout, 'Pack your trunks. You're both going with us.' The lassies hugged while squealin' ther thanks to ther fa."

The friends raised their mugs laughing at their little theatrical performance. The rest of the tavern's customers whistled and cheered demanding bows from the actors.

When James returned to Ramsay's loft, he pondered Mudie's plan. Remembering that the youngest five daughters were content to stay in Scotland with their mother and baby brother. James asked himself, why would those girls, only seventeen and eighteen years-old, be so eager to give up their comfortable home for such a wild place?

That night James' dreams took him to a barren landscape where he wandered in dense, fog. He couldn't see anything or anyone and felt alone. Fear gripped him as he struggled to find his way. He longed to see something familiar. He called for his Mother, for Will, for Mr. Ramsey. No one answered. He fell to his knees and sobbed into the palms of his hands.

Startled by a loud cry, James sat up on his cot listening. There was no sound. His heart was beating fast and he could barely catch his breath. Sweat dripped down his back. He swung his feet to the floor and pushed his damp hair off his forehead. *A dream. I remember now.*

He drank from the pitcher of water that sat on the stand next to the wash basin. He paced as quietly as he could, making sure he stepped over the floorboard that squeaked. He didn't want to disturb the Ramseys, but he needed to figure out what had spooked him. Going over the dream's scene he admitted to himself that he was worried about what would become of him when he finished his apprenticeship. He only had a few more weeks and he had no leads on a job or an idea of where he should go. He'd never thought about leaving Montrose, but the city wasn't big enough for more than one blacksmith.

Mudie's Plan

September 1684

Mudie, a man who achieved his goals through forward thinking, planning, and preparation, spent days contemplating his enterprise. During a meeting with his friend and attorney Thomas Gordon, Mudie asked, "What are your thoughts about indentured servants?" He leaned forward intent on Gordon's answer.

"Well, with indentures you know who you have before you arrive in America. Otherwise, there'll be the problem of finding willing, honest workers as soon as you land." Then Gordon surprised his friend, "You know my brother, John, is one of the proprietors of East New Jersey."

"Yes, of course." Mudie sat back in the straight-backed chair.

"He's retained me to represent him there in the town of Perth Amboy. I'll be taking the ship leaving Montrose November fifth this year."

Standing to leave Mudie smiled, "I just might be on that ship with you."

In deep thought Mudie walked down High Street, then onto George Street toward Baltic Street and his home. He took no notice of the bustle and noise in the busy thoroughfares. He wondered if funding workers' voyages and then bed and board for four years would be worth the investment. He decided he'd have to examine his ledgers and calculate the costs.

It took several days, but Mudie worked out the estimates. He could finance up to twelve indentured servants. But where, he thought, will I find twelve skilled, honest, hardworking people who'd go to America?

He outlined his needs, a strong man to oversee laborers and manage property, a woman housekeeper for the family home, a blacksmith, miller, and five men to clear land, construct a gristmill, house, plantation buildings, and farm the land. One woman would be suitable at the main house and three more for the plantation to spin, weave, sew, clean, cook, and manage kitchen gardens. Thirteen. He'd need to work something out.

During the next several weeks, providence seemed to open Mudie's eyes and ears. People he'd taken for granted he now saw as potential servants. Heartened, he hung a broad sheet on the public notice wall asking interested parties to apply through his attorney.

Mudie asked his miller John Loofborow to accompany him not as an indentured servant but as his employee. Loofborow agreed without hesitation. And that solved the problem of numbers. Mudie could still afford twelve indentured servants to fill his needs.

Servants from the Mudie household and businesses had frequented Blacksmith Ramsey's forge. They had tools repaired, wheels replaced, and other items made from iron. Mudie admired Aiden Ramsey and the care he took teaching his young apprentices the trade. He'd also noticed James Fitchett, the current apprentice. He liked the young man's cheerfulness and the prompt way he attended to customers' needs.

Not wanting to disrespect Ramsay, Mudie visited the blacksmith and inquired, "When will Fitchett complete his tenure?" And was pleased to hear the reply.

"End of next month. I don't know what he plans from there."

...

One cool crisp autumn day in late September Mudie approached James at Ramsay's forge and began, "James, Ramsay tells me you'll be a Master Blacksmith by late October."

"Yes Sir, that's right."

"I'm going to America in November and need a smithy. I think you'd fit the position. Would you—"

To Mudie's surprise James interrupted him with, "Yes, sir. Yes, I'll go." Mudie explained details, but James found it difficult to listen. He was already daydreaming of the great adventure.

After Mudie left, James smiled and clapped his calloused hands as he realized he'd been offered not only employment, but a free voyage and four-years of food and bed.

James had never made a decision for himself. His father, his widowed mother, his stepfather, Mr. Bell, and then Master Ramsay had directed his life from birth to this, his twenty-fourth year. Since his mother's death two years ago he'd worried, not knowing what he'd do after his apprenticeship. But at that moment he believed luck put his future before him. He was delighted that it hadn't taken any thought or searching on his part.

As soon as he finished his responsibilities for the day, James ran all the way to Mudie's stable. He arrived, panting. He leaned forward with his hands on his knees unable to speak.

Will greeted him with a huge smile and sparkling eyes. "James, Mr. Mudie's taking me to America. I'm happy to go, but I'll miss you, Mate."

"Don't worry," James nearly shouted as his smile grew wider, "I'm going, too."

Laughing, they clasped each other's upper arms sharing their enthusiasm.

■■■

Mudie's twelve-year old daughter Janet spent time out of doors whenever she could. She didn't like acting a proper lady making calls to neighbors and serving tea to guests. However, once her mother insisted that she accompany her to visit Mrs. Thomas Gordon, Janet couldn't be kept away. Ellen Gordon had married at seventeen and within five short years bore four children. She appreciated the time Janet spent in her home playing with the children. Over time, Janet acted not only as playmate to the young Gordons but became a genial companion to Ellen.

When Mudie announced what he called 'good news' Janet's heart sunk. Thomas Gordon planned to take his family to America on the same ship as her father. *I know I'll miss father. After all, he is my father. But how will I survive without Ellen and the children? How will they survive without me?*

...

November fifth, sixteen-eighty-four Janet wanted to stay in bed, but her mother insisted that she present herself properly, whatever that meant, at the dock to see the travelers off.

"Mama, I can't, I feel sick. I'll lose my breakfast on my good dress and then you'll be very unhappy with me. Please, just let me stay in bed."

"No, Janet. Ellen and the children need to see your smiling face as they sail off. You might be the last civilized creature they encounter. Do you want them to think you don't care for them after all the time you've spent together?"

Janet rolled out from under the down comforter and put her warm feet on the cold floorboards. "Burrrr," *Why would anyone get on a ship in the winter?* Wrapping her heavy robe around her shivering body she swore under her breath, "If father comes back in two years, as he promised, I'll make him take me to New Jersey. I need to be with Ellen and the children."

...

Turmoil abounded on the waterfront. Crowds of people milled around. Some pushing forward to find their way up the gang plank and others there to bid farewells. By some miracle, the passengers, with trunks and tools, the crew and cargo, all made it on the ship before the Captain's orders to weigh anchor.

Mudie's indentured servants found places for themselves below deck, then, all eighteen people in their party leaned against the outer rail and waved goodbye to family, friends, and homeland.

The ship's captain shouted orders. sailors ran every which way. Standing on the dock Janet didn't understand the activity, but she noticed the ship began to move toward the channel, toward the North Sea, toward America. She tried, how she tried, to put on the happy, 'proper' face her mother had demanded, but her heart sank watching the family she loved sail away. She feared she'd never see the Gordon family again. She managed to hold back tears, but her spirit crumbled.

James wondered if he'd miss Montrose. He wondered if anyone in Montrose would miss him.

The Thomas and Benjamin's ship's log listed those traveling with Mudie:

> *Indentured Servants: William and Elizabeth Burnett, Effie Streton, Catherine Maxlie, Margarett Symson, Andrew Mackemie, Robert Waber, George Johnstone, Margarett*

Gentleman, John Giddis, William Brodie, and
James Fitchett (blacksmith)

Employee: John Loofborow, Miller

Children: David, James, Elizabeth, and Isobel

...

Before leaving Scotland, Mudie had purchased two parcels of land in America. He carried drawn plans for a gristmill, blacksmith forge, and house to be built within the settlement of Perth Amboy, New Jersey. He would set up a plantation with a main house, servants' quarters, and outbuildings on the parcel of land that sat on the banks of South River.

The Thomas & Benjamin, although a small vessel, carried one-hundred-thirty people. That included the seamen, twenty-seven women, and six or seven children. During the long voyage great gusts of wind caused huge waves that tossed the ship about. Since James had never been to sea, it took several days for him to find what the sailors called 'sea legs.' His stomach churned for hours. Some days he chose hunger over vomiting. At first, he enjoyed the salty aroma of the sea, but after a month the wind couldn't blow strong enough to remove the reeking odors of rotting food or human and animal waste encased below deck. Even after dumping it overboard, the sickening stench added to everyone's distress.

Eighteen weeks after leaving Montrose, the crew sighted the American coast. At first, it appeared as trees growing out of the sea. However, the Captain identified the place as the middle of Long Island.

Everyone on board joined in, "Hip-hip-hooray! Hip-hip-hooray! Hip-hip-hooray!"

Towards nightfall the ship anchored near Sandy Hook, New Jersey. James' innards shivered. He thought he was eager to set foot on the strange new land, into his new life, but his stomach roiled. Fear gripped him at the thought of waiting savages.

The ship traveled to Perth Amboy the following morning. Passengers disembarked on a bitter, cold day in February sixteen-eighty-five. Snow and ice covered the trees, buildings, roads, and cleared land. Day's end brought a thick wet fog.

Damp, cold, and still queasy from fear, James examined the frozen scene before him. *Maybe I should've stayed in Scotland.* But the thought of another sea voyage to return led to his silent pledge, *I'll never leave dry land again.*

Bewildered, James said to Will, "When my mother sent me off to Ramsey's I thought I'd left the civilized world. Now look where I am."

Shaking his head in wonder, Will replied, "This time James, we're in a new world for sure."

Mudie Kept His Promise

September 1685

Once Mudie arrived in Perth Amboy, he hired extra laborers and jumped into making his venture profitable. He'd heard that arrivals in a settlement called Newark had begun work on a gristmill three years earlier and still hadn't completed it. His workers finished and he opened for business within just one month of his arrival.

The building thirty-two-feet-wide, and forty-feet-long, housed two rough stones made from local limestone. They each measured thirty-feet-in-diameter. One would sit on the mill's floor unmoving. Then raw kernels of wheat or corn would be dropped onto it from above. The top stone would be lowered onto the grain and then turn, breaking the grain down into flour.

A horse was harnessed to a wooden beam that was attached to a series of gears and pulleys. The horse walked in a large circle pushing the beams forward which set the machinery into action driving the movement of the upper stone. Since flour was the most important export back to England, Mudie looked forward to receiving business from the entire community.

The earth's sand, gravel, and clay made a good, rough building-stone. John Cockburn, a Scottish mason, used the claystone to build Mudie's renowned house, finishing it in less than two months.

The family enjoyed the six-room, two-story structure. Mudie even had a luxury not seen in most Perth Amboy homes, a study where he conducted business at a huge, oak desk crafted by a local carpenter. The house sat above a cellar and an attic room crowned the structure. Settlers could often be heard remarking on the beauty and soundness of the home's construction.

Mudie gave Issy and Margaret free rein to furnish and decorate the interior. Older women with many years of household experience couldn't have put together a more pleasant or comfortable home. Besides the furnishings purchased from local craftsmen, the girls surprised their men folk with mementos they'd brought from Montrose— miniature portraits of their Mother and those siblings who had stayed in Scotland, a candelabra separated from its match for the dining room table, and a wall hanging of dried heather pressed under glass. Items that invoked special memories in each of the transplanted family members.

Margaret even used her feminine wiles on a grieving widower before he returned to Scotland. He didn't want to take his late wife's small harpsichord on another sea voyage. Margaret haggled with him until he gave in to a sum well under its value. He hoped his wife would forgive him, but he had no other offers and he did admire Margaret's zeal for its good tone and beautiful carved wooden case. After his daily efforts Mudie found contentment during evenings sitting near the hearth listening to Margaret play his favorite music on her new prized possession.

While laborers toiled on the house and mill, Mudie had sent his sons, Junior and James, to the plantation acreage on South River by Duck Creek. Mudie wrote his wife: I sent the boys to the plantation with seven indentured servants, six strong horses, one ox, and a swine, which I think good enough for the first year of a plantation.

Mudie wanted planting done early, hoping for an abundant wheat harvest in early autumn. He visited the plantation often, but Junior had full management of the land and servants. Mudie trusted his son to act as his proxy.

By the end of his first year in America, a list of successful Perth Amboy merchants would include the name of David Mudie. He would also be appointed a lay-Judge of a local court.

In the fall of sixteen-eighty-five, only six-months since his arrival Mudie sat in his dimly lit and sparsely decorated study with his friend Thomas Gordon. Mudie took a quaff of ale, and then complained, "If we don't find a way to collect rents from the land leases, our investment will fail. This whole venture will be a disaster. And Isobel will never let me forget it."

"What can we do? If Governor Barkley won't enforce the law, our hands are tied." Gordon looked at the tall mug of dark liquid he held. "As judges we can rule on matters at court, but we can't enforce payment. We have to act within the laws the proprietors wrote into their constitution for this land."

Mudie rubbed his round, gurgling belly, a sign of some after-dinner discomfort, "Well, I need capital. The mill and blacksmith shop are doing well, but I'm still supporting twelve indentured servants."

Taking in Mudie's ale and his host's concerns, Gordon agreed, "I could use more income, too. Raising four children with another on the way is taking a toll on my savings."

Walking to the window, Mudie looked out at the soupy-fog settling in and continued, "I've been studying the situation. It seems to me settlers will continue to find their way here. I'm thinking of using the last of my capital to buy more Proprietary shares of land."

Gordon straightened in his chair, "You want to work more land? You'd need more servants."

Turning back to face his friend Mudie explained, "Oh, no, not land to improve, land to sell at a profit. Then with that increase I'd buy more land to resell. I believe buying and selling will provide more of an increase than holding the land and trying to collect rents as the proprietors insist on doing."

As he settled back into his chair Gordon mumbled, "I hadn't thought of that, but you might have something. I'll have to think it through."

■■■

1686

37

Jan Brinkerhoff, a barrel-chested man with a jolly disposition, lived with his family in The Netherlands' city of Haarlem, a thriving industrial hub known for its linen weaving, bleaching, and finishing. An independent weaver, he managed a modest-sized workshop behind his house. He bought processed hemp from farmers which his wife, Lijsbeth, a petite, quiet, but steady woman, with her few hired women spun into yarn. Jan also employed a handful of men to help him weave that into broad sheets of linen fabric. His eldest daughter, Sarah assisted by her younger brothers Hans and Izaak, bleached the cloth and then hung it on tenterhooks to stretch and dry.

One evening, as Sarah returned to the house from the privy, she overheard her father speak to his wife in an unusually quiet voice, "I have a foreboding, Wife, and I fear for our livelihood. You know for years buyers have been eager to acquire our family's fine linen but talk lately has it that the exporters are getting greedy and want higher profits. Some have contracted with workers in rural areas where labor is cheaper."

Without looking up from her needle threading she said, "Maybe the talk you've heard is just that, talk."

Sure, that neither parent heard her tread on the steps, Sarah stopped to listen from a vantage point where she could also see them.

"No, I know it's the truth. It's happening. We're going to lose our customers and in time, our business. I'm afraid to just sit here and wait for the inevitable." After a few puffs on his pipe he asked, "What say you about setting up our shop in America?"

"America?" Lijsbeth's eyes widened as she yelped, dropped her sewing, and sucked her punctured fingertip.

As if not noticing her reaction he went on, "Yes, I've been reading about New Netherlands and I think we could do well there. The Dutch there would appreciate our linen, remind them of home."

"Do they harvest hemp in America? You need hemp to make linen."

"I know that, woman. How could a country expect to grow, let alone thrive, without linen to clothe its people?" Jan puffed on his pipe relaxing with the sweet flavor of the tobacco.

Bleeding stopped, Lijsbeth continued with her mending, "Maybe they don't use linen. Maybe they dress in wild animal furs and hides like the Indians I've heard about in that new world."

"Don't be silly. The Dutch are there. It's a civilized land."

Sounding more like a parent speaking to a child than a wife to a husband Lijsbeth finished, "Well, Jan, you best pray about it and follow God's plan. He's the one in charge, you know."

Sarah tiptoed up the last flight of stairs to her attic room. She gasped for air as she laid upon her narrow cot and pulled the quilt to her chin. *Father can't possibly be serious. I'm to marry Wilhelm here in this Netherlands not in any new world.*

She normally loved the solitude of her small room, but that night the walls seemed to press in on her. Her chin trembled. She shivered, unaccustomed to fear. *Oh, God, what will become of me? Please guide my father in your righteousness.* Usually after prayer, Sarah drifted off to a peaceful sleep, however, that fateful night she tossed and turned until dawn.

...

A few days later Jan announced his decision to the family. They were going to the New World. No moans or pleas from his children could sway his determination. He had a plan.

The three oldest, Sarah, twenty, Hans seventeen, and fifteen-year-old Izaak were released from their work in the family shop and sent to cash paying employment in the city. Evenings they completed their family chores. Dogged in his resolution to take his family to America he forbade them to socialize declaring, "No courting." No need for him to concern himself, they were much too exhausted.

Sarah hardly found time to speak with Wilhelm on Sundays after church services. Her father assured her that her betrothed would join them on the new continent, but she still worried. Of course, she didn't complain, it was her duty to obey.

Brinkerhoff sold everything he could, even his loom. He wanted to build one from his adopted land's forest. Lijsbeth, however, insisted on taking her spinning wheel. They packed only necessary items. Jan, never a cultivator, planned to maintain his family on a small farm while weaving settler's linen.

The entire family worked and prayed, scrimped, and saved to reach his goal. Soon the money was gathered and the family exhausted, but Brinkerhoff's enthusiasm hadn't waned. Still determined to fulfill his dream in America, he bought a small piece of land in now English owned Eastern New Jersey. He'd heard that many Scots had immigrated there, and it was true that The Netherlands and Scotland carried on healthy trade between the two countries. He didn't think it would be difficult to live among them even though he spoke only Dutch.

■■■

June 1686

With the mill and plantation in good hands, Mudie kept his promise and returned to Scotland.

Mudie's blacksmith James hadn't seen a barber since arriving in Perth Amboy. His hair had grown to cover his eyebrows and reach his collar. Pacing he used both hands to push his fine hair off his forehead. *I'm only half-way through my indentured contract.* He worried, many questions running through his thoughts. Did Mudie hope to bring the rest of his family back to New Jersey or did he plan to stay in Scotland? What will happen to me if Mudie doesn't return? Would he sell me to another settler? Or return me to Scotland?

His stomach churned. Or, bloody-hell, would Mudie give me my independence with a debt hanging over my head—a debt it might take me years to pay? James had months to fret about his future.

···

August 1686

A maid greeted Mudie after he knocked on the heavy oak door of his Montrose home. No one came running to greet him. The woman taking his coat whispered that the mistress was in the sitting room. Smiling broadly Mudie entered the room and walked to his wife's side. He gently kissed her check.

Without even a hello to her husband, she whispered, "Where are the children, David? Why didn't you bring them back to me?" Tears rolled down her face. "I'm certain all four wanted to return home."

"I gave them the choice, Isobel. They're busy and didn't want to take time away from their endeavors. They send their love to you all."

"Well, I feel abandoned . . ." dabbing her face with a lace trimmed linen hanky she went on, "I . . . I am dismayed at their decision to remain in the land of savages. I thought they'd miss their mother, and of course, the children left behind. I can't imagine why they didn't come home. Have you turned them into uncaring ruffians?"

"No, my dear," controlling his temper at her accusations, he patted her arm, noticing the considerable weight she'd gained in his absence, "They are the same gentle, loving children they've always been."

Mudie was grateful that his wife and younger children were in good circumstances. His mill and shop had supported them well. That evening at dinner, the children appeared to be glad to have him home as they excitedly planned outings and socials to acquaint him with what he had missed.

As often as he attempted to explain his success to Isobel, she'd change the subject or leave the room. Every day Mudie reminded himself to be patient and listen to his family's renditions of life in Montrose. He didn't want to overpower them with his exploits in New Jersey. Although, he was sure once they heard of his successes, they'd want to join him and reunite the family. Very soon, he understood that Isobel was even more determined to stay in Scotland. She had no intention of changing her mind. Yet, whenever Mudie considered staying in Montrose and abandoning America, he fell into depths of self-doubt and despair.

He visited Dr. John Gordon often to help quell those feelings. As a friend, John expressed sympathy for Mudie's predicament. As an investor, anxious to hear about East New Jersey's Proprietary venture, John listened for hours. Mudie could see pleasure in John's face hearing of the many improvements that settlers had made. It was no wonder Gordon continued to encourage Mudie's return.

After several weeks of debating with himself, Mudie decided he couldn't stay in Scotland. He couldn't give up the adventure and opportunities waiting in New Jersey.

Approaching Isobel as she worked on needlepoint in the sitting room, Mudie pleaded, "Isobel, please come to America with me. I promise I'll book passage for you anytime you want to visit Scotland. I need you with me."

Without looking up from her hoop and yarns she answered as if speaking to a young child, "David, dear, I have told you many times, I will not go. Now, leave it be. I'm busy."

Frustrated by her stubbornness, he escalated his plea, "You must go with me. Wives are to obey and follow their husbands." Getting no reply drove him over the edge, red in the face he shouted, "Why are you so obstinate?"

"David, calm yourself. I will not go, and you cannot force me. I have given you eleven children and have been a good wife, but this is my home. This is where I belong. I will not leave. If you must follow your foolish notions, go. You may want to die in an uncivilized land, but I will die in my homeland. Now, please for the last time, I'm asking you to leave me be."

"Your decision saddens me, but I am returning to New Jersey." A beaten man he retreated to his study. Each stubborn spouse refused to give in to the other.

Although Mudie's fourteen-year-old daughter, Janet, had begun preparing for her entry into Montrose society, she begged her parents to allow her to go to Perth Amboy. Janet and Ellen Gordon exchanged letters, but Janet wanted more. The Gordon family had been blessed with two infants since they landed in New Jersey. How would she ever know those children without leaving Scotland? "Mother, please let me go with father. Ellen needs me, and I miss the children so." Janet begged.

"Your father, in his haughtiness and self-importance, is leaving me again. Leave me be. I don't want to speak to anyone."

"But, Mother, please."

"Janet, I refuse to discuss this with you or your father. I don't care what you do." A mother's bitter words thrown at her daughter.

The young girl sobbed as she ran to her room.

Mudie saw himself as ineffective as a mill without a great stone. He didn't know what to do. He wanted to make both Isobel and Janet happy, but couldn't see how.

A gloom permeated the house and its inhabitants as he prepared to leave. Consumed with his own anguish, he didn't notice anyone else in the family so, on the day of his return voyage, he was surprised to find Janet waiting in his carriage, her trunk and valise stowed ready to go.

On a rainy September day, Janet and her father sailed to New Jersey and Isobel remained in Montrose. Husband and wife would exchange amiable, and at times, affectionate letters, but never meet again.

October 1686

Mudie's son Junior had stood in for his father but stayed at the plantation in South River. James had managed to solve problems and handle emergencies at the forge, but, with Mudie back and at least the next two-years of his life secure, he could spend more time with Will and his other friends.

Reunited with Ellen Gordon and all her children, Janet Mudie's countenance radiated happiness. Janet read to Ellen's children and helped teach their lessons. She kept them safe when outdoors playing tag or rolling in piles of colorful crunchy autumn leaves. The children introduced Janet to their Lenape Indian neighbors and Janet joined in learning the native's games and listening to their folk lore. Janet remembered her mother's fears about the savages and was surprised that these natives welcomed the settlers and lived peacefully among them.

Everyone counted on one another. So, it was natural that in late November when Ellen Gordon and her four oldest children became ill, the community stepped in delivering hearty soups.

Day and night Margaret and Issy bathed fevered brows with cool, damp cloths. Janet read to the children and made up stories with happy endings. Two young Indian children brought their medicine by dancing on the hard earth, sometimes damp from rain or light snow, and chanting near the Gordon's home. In their own ways, Scots and Natives prayed for their friends' recovery.

The Gordons' health varied from day to day. One day they'd appear to be recovering and join conversations, but then without warning they'd slump back into fever and delirium. The youngest two whimpered in their sleep. A wet nurse offered her breasts, but at times the babes were too weak to suckle. Everything that could be done for the ailing children had been done, but in vain. One by one neighbors carried the four small coffins to St. Peter's burial grounds.

Ellen Gordon's constitution had never been strong, and grief weakened her even more. On December twelfth she died in her sleep while her husband held her hand. His broad shoulders collapsed as he prayed fervently for his two infants, but within a fortnight, the babes followed their mother and siblings in death.

■■■

Dressed in their heavy great coats, Will and James made their way through the frigid evening, down Water Street, and into the Blue Moon Tavern, Perth Amboy's meeting place of off-duty servants. After warming themselves at the hearth, Will ordered an ale and James a cider as they scanned the dusky room for familiar faces. Before they could even find a servant girl to flirt with, they heard a woman crying. Turning toward the sound, they recognized Catherine Maxlie, another of Mudie's indentured servants blubbering into a crumpled rag.

Neither Will nor James recognized the girl sitting with her, but they heard her ask, "Cathy, what's got you so upset?"

No one could mistake Cathy's distinctive speech. Wiping at her nose she exclaimed, "It's . . . it's . . . Miss Janet."

Concerned the girl asked, "Miss Janet? What's happened to her? Is she Ill?"

"No. No. Her body is well, but her spirit is broke. She is inconsolable since Misses Gordon and her children passed. Miss Janet don't eat nor come out of her room. I fear she wants to join them."

"Hear. Hear. Now. Don't get yourself sick with worry." Pushing a mug of ale in front of Cathy, her friend went on, "Drink this, it'll help you calm down. Come on now, it's our day off. No time for crying. Clean your face and let's have some fun."

James shuffled his feet and finished his cider. As he backed away from the bar he said, "Let's get out of here."

Will took a last swallow of ale and followed back into the cold night air and into the street.

As they walked, James remarked, "I've been wondering why Mudie hadn't been around much of late. What have you heard from the house servants?"

"They say Mudie's worried sick for his daughter but doesn't know what to do for her."

"And I imagine he's concerned for his friend's loss."

"Aye," Will agreed, "Gordon must be undone losing his family like that."

Hanging his head, James shared his thoughts, "I wonder if the marriage bed is worth the pain. My mother was so happy until my father drowned. And how is Mudie doing without his wife here with him? It doesn't seem to bother him."

Will chuckled, "Maybe he's happier with her in Scotland. She could be sharp tongued and overbearing."

"But what's the point of marrying if you're going to be unhappy either living with a wife or losing her?"

"I don't know. So far I haven't found a woman to share my bed and I guess I won't here in Perth Amboy."

"Why do you say that? There are a few good women here."

"Yes, there are, although I've not found one, I'd want to be with longer than a few hours. But Loofborow is leaving Mudie's employ to start a mill in Piscataway. He's buying the remainder of my indenture contract and taking me with him."

Stopping in his tracks, James turned to Will, "Bloody Hell, mate, will I ever see you again?"

"I don't know," Will shrugged his shoulders. "Maybe once our contracts are satisfied."

Investments

January 1687

Late one night, feeling at loose ends and bundled in his great coat with his warm hat and his scarf wrapped tightly around his neck, James wandered the deserted city streets. He walked from High Street to Market then unto Water Street toward the docks. After two years in Perth Amboy he still found himself looking for he knew not what. He had time, but with Will gone the past month, he had no interest in going to the Blue Moon.

Some days thoughts of life with a woman wouldn't leave James' mind. He'd flirted with servant girls but found none he wanted to share his company with away from the tavern. The women seemed either too silly or burdened with sadness. Many of them voiced fears of being marooned in a strange land. They talked of their homeland, but never about a future in America.

He asked himself, what kind of woman do I want to marry? Not a frivolous one, or a gloomy one for sure. Did he even want to marry? The chance of failure or loss weighed heavy on his mind. Maybe it'd be best to remain alone.

He missed his parents, Montrose, and the carefree life he once had. He missed his good mate Will, too.

February 1687

During their voyage Lijsbeth became ill. The family prayed for her return to health not knowing if seasickness or influenza had attacked. Sarah tended to her two young sisters, Nora and Emily, and prepared food for the family. Sarah's mother had taught her well, and Sarah could fill Lijsbeth's place.

The family found walking, eating, and even sleeping difficult with continuous movement of the ship swaying to and fro. Sarah, too afraid to use any kind of fire, gave up on bathing herself or her sisters. Laundering clothing was impossible and what they ate, they ate cold. There were many days when no one consumed anything due to seasickness.

•••

Janet remained despondent for several weeks. Her sisters prayed she'd accept her loss and return to her normal self. Helping Ellen had given Janet's life meaning. Since her friend's death her life seemed useless and empty. She prayed every night for relief. Then one day her prayers seemed to be answered. Janet awoke with new purpose. Her duty to Ellen meant helping Mr. Gordon through his desperate grief. After contemplating her neighbor's needs and her abilities, she wrote out a plan.

Janet joined her family for breakfast donning a well-worn day-dress. Happy to see her they kept quiet. None of them felt comfortable talking about tender feelings. As she chewed her last bite of toast, she wiped her mouth and ran from the dining room. The family sat stunned as they heard her call, "I'll be home later," and slam the front door. Without slowing she arrived at the Gordon home to begin her responsibilities.

Janet barged in with a melodic greeting for the cook, as she stomped snow from her fur-lined boots. "Good morning, Lucy. I hope you're well today."

"Yes, Ma'am, Miss Janet, Ah feel tip top." Lucy, a short, stocky woman, answered in her thick Scottish brogue.

"That's fine. Are you preparing hearty foods for your master?"

"Yes, Ma'am. You know Ah've been takin' care-a Mr. Gordon loch his missus hud me dae."

Janet hung her heavy coat on the hook by the door, "Good. He needs to regain his strength."

"Yes Ma'am, Ah know."

Janet pulled her back straight to her full height wishing she were taller, more grown-up looking. "Lucy, I need you to swear to me that you can keep a secret."

The woman who was old enough to be Janet's mother, looked at the girl with a bit of suspicion, she asked, "Whit kin' ay secrit dae ye hae?"

"I don't want Mr. Gordon's home to cause him any more grief than he has already from losing his beloved wife." Janet wiped a tear forming in her eye. "And I know you've been left with extra work here."

"Yes um." Lucy nodded and sat down at the wooden table near the hearth. She put her hands in her lap and listened to Janet's ideas. "Fine, Miss Janet, Ah will nae say a wood."

52

Janet sounded a little harsher than she intended as she emphasized her thoughts, "Not to anyone."

"No. I mean, yes. Ma'am. Nae a body."

"Thank you, Lucy, I know I can count on you." She smiled her relief. "Now, where do I start?

Lucy, adjusted her cap, smoothed down her apron and went back to scrubbing the cook area. Janet tidied up the house swinging a broom to chase spider webs, dust, and dirt from ceiling to floor. With tears in her eyes, she wiped little fingerprints from the windows. Late in the afternoon, before leaving, Janet set the table and placed Mr. Gordon's books and pipes on the table at his armchair.

Once a week she scrubbed the floors, when the sun was out and the wind calm, she beat the rugs. She even had her family's housekeeper, Mrs. Burnett, help her stitch cushions and stuff them with goose down for the seat and back of Mr. Gordon's chair. Each week she brushed Gordon's suits, mended socks, and secured buttons just as she had watched Ellen do. Following Ellen's example Janet learned to do whatever needed to be done.

When spring arrived, Janet planted a garden and tended it fondly remembering how Ellen had loved her flowers. She pulled weeds and carried water to the garden's parched ground. Like Ellen, she kept fresh-cut blossoms in the vase on Mr. Gordon's dinner table.

At first, engrossed in his grief Gordon didn't notice his surroundings. He walked through life like a ghost, eating, sleeping, and working without feeling or thinking about his loss. However, in time, the dark cloud of gloom began to lift. He enjoyed the tidy comfort of his home, soft cushions, and flowers. His pipe and book always at hand. He assumed the cook had added the extra domestic touches and would soon tire of the effort.

Instead, his home continued to be maintained at his wife's standards. After several months, he approached his cook. "Lucy, you've outdone yourself. You keep up the house and garden and still provide delicious meals. I don't know how you do it, but I want you to know I appreciate it. I'll see to a bit of a raise for you."

"Sir, i'd loch tae tak' credit, but it isnae me bin daein' th' extra wark an' fancyin' up." She stood still looking at the floor, afraid to make eye contact with her master.

Puzzled lines appeared on Gordon's face, "Who then? I haven't authorized you to hire help."

"Nae, sairrr, an' i've nae hired help. Sir." She couldn't look him in the eyes.

"Lucy, don't just stand there staring at the floor, woman, who has been helping you?"

"Sorry, sairrr, but Ah bin asked tae keep it tae myself, sir."

Gordon could feel his ire rising but managed to control himself. "But now, I'm demanding to know. What stranger has been coming into my home and intruding on my privacy? You must tell me. Now."

Lucy cleared her throat and wiped at her eyes, "A trust is a trust, sairrr, but seein' yoo're sae upsit. it's Miss Janet Mudie who's bin here every day, sir."

In disbelief he asked, "Janet Mudie? She's just a child. How could she manage? How could she know what's needed?"

"Ah can't answer those questions, aw Ah ken she's th' a body bin workin' here every day. She has, sairrr. She said she's daein' it fur 'er frend. Yer late guidwife, bless 'er sool."

Gordon sat in his chair dumbfounded and baffled.

···

Early on Janet had enlisted her father to invite Mr. Gordon to Sunday dinners so he wouldn't have to fend for himself on his cook's day off. The next dinner after Lucy's confession, Gordon saw Janet through new eyes. He watched for any nuance that would give away her secret. He couldn't find any difference in her behavior. She was as she always had been, a cheerful, fun-loving child.

I should thank her and dismiss her from the burden she's stepped into. But as he saw the sparkle in her eyes. He remembered how sad she'd been after Ellen's death and he couldn't bring himself to confront her.

Thomas Gordon's brother John was a proprietor of East New Jersey and as his representative Thomas wrote to him whenever business dictated.

April 1687

John, my brother, and friend,

*Thank you for your condolences. My heart continues
to ache at the loss of my loving wife and children. I
work as much as my physical body allows for as I
work, I am freed of the overbearing grief.*

*Notwithstanding my personal circumstances, I must
write with troubling news of East New Jersey. I know
you expect to hear of success for the plantations and
rent payments. I can indeed, tell you that settlers
continue arriving and are improving the land.
However, they refuse to pay their rents. Governor
Barclay doesn't want to agitate unrest. Therefore, he
refuses to enforce payments.*

*Of late, the Province has another dilemma. King
James II sent one Edmund Andros to oversee his New
York holdings and this Andros has assumed the same
position over New Jersey. Barclay refuses to leave
office causing contention and confusion for the
populous and the governing bodies. The Proprietors'
Group must bring this situation under control before
tempers rise into aggression and riots.*

*I await instructions from you to put a stop to this
tyranny.*

Yours — Thomas

...

Finally, Brinkerhoff's' voyage came to an end, the exhausted family disembarked on a lovely, sunny, spring-day into much confusion and noise as fellow passengers swarmed toward their new lives. Sarah watched as her father studied the area. She'd never seen him hesitate. To her he seemed a man of action. She and her brothers had learned some English on the ship, yet they didn't attempt to ask strangers for help.

∎∎∎

Since James arrived in Perth Amboy each day passed into another, days into months, months into two years. His life hadn't changed much until the spring day his master sent him to the docks to deliver a sea captain's repaired chain. The view of the sea with the aroma of salt air and fresh-caught fish always swept James' soul back to his Scottish seaport of Montrose. He missed his parents and the comfortable home he'd known with them.

The seagulls' shrieks drew James' attention and he remembered how as a child their loud calls had joined with his excitement as he ran to the dock to meet his father returning from a sea voyage. He recalled wondering what the birds could see as they glided through the air above him. There in Perth Amboy he knew that the gulls could see the docks, the city, and a few cabins in the thick forest beyond.

He figured they could see the Lenape Indian camps, Sandy Hook, the Raritan River, and the ferry going from Perth Amboy to Staten Island. He wondered as they flew higher if the gulls could see all of Staten Island and even New York City where ships from all over the world docked. James had never been out of New Jersey, but he had heard about Staten Island and New York City's busy harbor.

While James daydreamed and reminisced, his eyes wandered over the scene. Noticing movement and hearing a commotion, he turned and saw people disembarking from one of the ships docked there. He watched, remembering the day his feet touched the New World for the first time—intense fear had mixed with excitement as he had speculated what his future as an indentured blacksmith would hold in the new world.

He could easily recognize the difference between indentured servants with their masters and families or individuals traveling alone. He noticed a large family. A husband, wife and five children. The oldest, a slim girl who was a bit shorter than him and, he guessed, a little younger than his twenty-seven years, helped her parents. She had a high forehead, thick dark hair, and deep brown eyes. She seemed a little shy but had a beautiful smile.

Two girls probably eight and five-years-old clutched their older sister's skirt, fear in their eyes. Two boys not quite men, still looked uncomfortable with their long limbs, stared at their surroundings. The group didn't have many possessions. They appeared bewildered.

James approached the group slowly, holding his hat. To show respect, he kept his eyes and attention on the head of the family. "Excuse me, sir, may I assist you? Do you need directions to your destination?"

Sarah watched the young man as he spoke. His sandy-colored hair fell across his forehead. He was not slim like Wilhelm. He had muscular arms but wasn't as broad as her father either. He had a cheerful countenance and his eyes shone with kindness. She understood his determination to give aid to her father.

Jan looked at James with questioning eyes. He answered in Dutch and James couldn't understand what he said, but he motioned for the man to follow him and walked into a shop. The rope maker spoke both Dutch and English. James asked the merchant to please tell him what the man needed. The merchant greeted the newcomer in Dutch which brought a wide smile to the stranger's worried-looking face. James could see at least some anxiety slip away as he watched the two Dutchmen converse for several minutes.

The merchant then turned to James and explained, "This is Mr. Jan Brinkerhoff. He just arrived from Holland, he has a patent for farmland and needs to go to the land office to get directions to his parcel."

"Thank you for your help. Please assure Mr. Brinkerhoff that I can take him to the land office on my way back to the forge."

Hearing the translation, Mr. Brinkerhoff smiled and shook his head in the universal sign of agreement. He thanked the merchant and motioned for James to lead the way.

Sarah's New World

Although a year had passed since Will left Perth Amboy, James hadn't found another close mate to spend his free time with. Instead, a restless young man, James spent Sundays exploring the wilderness outside the settlement.

He learned to sit quietly and wait for wildlife to come near. Once in awhile he would see a young Lenape boy tracking game. Spring and summer James watched the birds flitting through the branches of the tall trees. He watched robins, red-winged blackbirds, blue jays, and small chickadees build nests and hunt food for their young. He heard red-billed woodpeckers pecking for insects in the trees while deer munched leaves from below and squirrels scurried to hide their supply of winter nuts and seeds. In the autumn huge ancient oaks and red maples turned vibrant golden-yellow and brilliant scarlets.

He hiked passed fertile land outside of Perth Amboy. Farmers grew hay, wheat, barley, vegetables, and a couple even had fruit trees. As the sun moved toward the west and brought evening, the owls hooted while grouse and wild turkey scampered through the thick brush.

That June, as James returned to Perth Amboy after one of his Sunday walks, he noticed a small roughly built cabin with chickens pecking for worms and seeds around the yard. He could hear children playing in the nearby woods. Approaching the cabin, James recognized the man relaxing in the yard enjoying his pipe. It was the Dutchman he'd helped. James could see that the land had been cleared, but he didn't know how the large family found room enough to lie down to sleep in the tiny cabin. Besides a few chickens, there was a vegetable garden, and a milk-cow.

The Dutchman signaled James to approach. He seemed happy to see a familiar face. Between Dutch, English, and hand signals the two men were able to conduct a simple conversation.

Sarah heard her father talking with someone. When curiosity got the best of her, she peeked out the window and saw the young man who'd come to their aid on the docks. She heard her father call his wife from the cabin to greet James. As soon as Lijsbeth saw him, she broke into a bright smile and invited James to join them for supper which he eagerly accepted. Sarah supposed he'd been enjoying the aroma of the hearty stew cooking on the wood stove.

Oh, no. I must look a fright. Sarah ran to the bucket of water kept in the cooking area and poured some into the wash bowl. She grabbed a bar of her mother's homemade soap and scrubbed her face. She smoothed her damp hands over her hair making sure there were no wayward strands then rubbed the front of her skirt to remove any dust or threads.

Her father brought the young man into the cabin. She greeted him in Dutch forgetting any English she'd learned. She could feel a flush cover her.

During supper, in halting English, pointing to himself, then the rest of his family, Hans, the fifteen-year-old, asked James, "Teach English?"

James exaggeratedly nodded his head signifying his willingness. "Yes. Yes."

Lessons began immediately. Pointing to his chest the man said "J-aa-mss. James." Once the family could repeat 'J-aa-mss' he pointed to each of them to learn their names.

Whenever he directed his attention to Sarah she blushed. And she noticed that every time that happened, James smiled and looked pleased with himself. Hans and Izaak shouted Dutch words while they mimed actions. Everyone laughed as James attempted to learn their language by copying them. Surrounded by James' laughter and good humor Sarah soon forgot herself and joined in the fun.

As she retired that evening, she was joyful for the first time since arriving in America. She thanked God for sending James to their home. Then, scolding herself for almost forgetting, asked God's blessing on her family and Wilhelm.

...

After just a few visits James found himself thinking of Sarah all week long. He wondered if she ever thought about him. Wanting to spend more time with her, he returned home by way of the Brinkerhoff cabin every week, always a welcomed guest at their table.

One Sunday James garnered his courage and walked to the cabin earlier than usual. He wanted to ask Sarah to join him on his walk. At the last moment he included her siblings in the invitation. All five were happy to go with him. James didn't mind, being with all of them didn't take away from time with Sarah. He didn't know why, but just being with her kept him smiling.

During their walks James taught the Brinkerhoff brood English and in return learned Dutch from them. Hello – *Hallo*. How are you? *Hoe gaat het*? Have a good day. *Nog een prestige dag toegewerist*. Thank you. *Dank u*. Sarah's brothers and sisters, eager to be with James, campaigned and won permission to get together with James every Sunday. On inclement days, the group remained in the Brinkerhoff cabin each practicing their new language skills.

Within a short time, communication became easier. On one of their walks James sang a Scottish song. The boys understood enough of the words to be embarrassed. They laughed and rough-housed with each other, especially when James got to the sixth verse:

I took the gold pin frae the scarf on my bosom,
And said, "Tak' ye this, in remembrance o' me."
And bravely I kissed the sweet lips o' the lassie
And I parted frae her on the road to Dundee.

Sarah blushed and chided James for his irreverent use of music. "In The Netherlands singing is only to worship God and thank Him for blessings."

She sang her favorite hymn:

Wilt heden nu treden voor God den Heere,
Hem boven al loven van herten seer,
End' maken groot zijins lieven namens eere,
Die daar nu onsen vijan slat terneer

We gather together to ask the Lord's blessing.
He chastens and hastens His will to make known.
The wicked oppressing now cease from distressing.
Sing praises to His Name; He forgets not His own.

Then explained its significance to her people, "The hymn was written to celebrate the Dutch victory at the battle of Turn Hout. The Dutch were fighting for their freedom against Catholic King Phillip II of Spain. Translated the title is 'We Gather Together' and the words convey thankfulness that, free from King Phillip, Protestants could worship in public, which they were not allowed to do under his rule. It was a glorious time in Dutch Protestant history."

From then on whenever James sang "On the Road to Dundee" Sarah sang "We Gather Together." They sang and laughed, teasing, but also showing acceptance of their differences.

James entertained the family with funny stories, but he never spoke of his family or life before New Jersey. His eyes had not lied that first day. He was a kind man, gentle, and eager to please. But he didn't attend church. Sarah accepted her parents' beliefs that a person's outward acts of religion assured his status as God's Elect. She feared for James' soul. And her own if she let feelings overrule her good judgement.

John Gordon corresponded with his brother Thomas with issues pertaining to the proprietors and their investments.

August 1687

Thomas,

I'm sure you have heard that James II fled England last year when William III, the Dutch King, invaded. With that change, we proprietors were able to order Andros out of New Jersey.

Please keep me abreast of the local reactions to Barclay's authority returned.

Sincerely — John

Decisions

September 1687

After a few weeks, a physical yearning strange to him drew James to Sarah's side. He wanted to touch her, but any such action would be crossing a line. He didn't want to anger her father or show disrespect to her. His heart fluttered and his knees went weak when she smiled at him and when she sang her hymns his heart almost burst.

James wanted to kiss Sarah and hold her close to him, but they were always chaperoned by her sisters or brothers. Inexperienced as he was, he didn't know what to do to alleviate his agony. He stopped taking his walks and spent Sunday's sitting under a tree by his cabin playing melancholy tunes on his tin whistle. He thought not seeing Sarah would help, but of course it didn't. In fact, not seeing her left him devastated.

Mudie, James' master, noticed his slumped shoulders and sad expression. He approached and asked, "Is everything all right? Do you need something? Is there something I can do to help?"

James tried to convince Mudie that he had no problems, but his employer persisted until James gave in and told him how he had been spending his days off and about the strong, confusing feelings he had for Sarah. In total hopelessness,

James admitted that he didn't know what to do to relieve the pain in his heart.

Holding back a chuckle, Mudie assured him, "You're all right, James. All young men go through this. Sounds to me like you want to bed her. Some folk call it love."

James face burned. He stuttered, "Love f-feels like th-this? My parents always looked happy and content."

"That's because they acted on their love in the marriage bed. How do you think you came about?"

"So, what do I do?" James asked with a sigh.

"Do you want to marry her? You have another year on your indenture contract. I remember warning you men about getting tangled up with women while you were under my contract. Do you have money to buy yourself free?"

"No, sir, I don't, and I do remember the warning. I'm not intending to break the deal."

"You've been an honest hard worker for me, James. I suppose if you decide to marry and can't wait, I could give you permission. But as part of such an arrangement you'd have to stay as a wage earner after your contract ends. We can discuss terms if it comes to that."

"Thank you, sir. I'll sort it and let you know."

That night James couldn't sleep. His mind questioned, could this be love? He thought about the relationship his parents had enjoyed. They seemed happy just being in the same room. They engaged in lengthy discussions about local events. They worked together to obtain their dreams. They enjoyed music, dancing, reading and were always observing what Mother called 'God's creations.' They especially enjoyed watching wee lads and lassies as they became aware of the world around them. His parents involved themselves in the Montrose community, but they were the happiest in their home together with him.

He saw his parents kiss, but he couldn't imagine that they had the strong urges he experienced when he thought about Sarah. But then he remembered his favorite bedtime story. It told how his parents met. His father turned it into a funny story, but his mother's rendition was a romantic fairy tale. As she told it . . .

Once upon a time in an enchanted village by the sea a beautiful and delicate young woman named Euphemia lived in a lovely stone house with her parents. Her father, a successful merchant, was able to give her the best of everything. The young woman had many acquaintances and parties to attend.

Euphemia was a special girl who would marry a wealthy man and raise a large family. Her children would be educated and have music and parties in their lives. They would wear fine clothing and want for nothing. These were the girl's deepest desires as she grew into womanhood. Many young men were eager to court her, but she found no one of interest.

Her eighteenth birthday was a beautiful spring Saturday. She wore her favorite white muslin dress. It had yellow ribbons weaved through the bodice with layers of ruffles cascading over the skirt from waist to hem. It was short enough to walk without tripping

*on the fabric, but long enough to cover her ankles.
The matching yellow ribbons and wide brim of her
hat flapped in the breeze.*

*It had rained that morning, but the grey clouds were
being pushed southwesterly on a light breeze from
the sea. The sun's bright rays warmed the air as each
cloud drifted away. Watching the world open from
the harshness of winter into the newness of spring
enlivened her.*

*Fat Robin Redbreasts pecked at the ground in search
of worms. Goldfinch called to their mates. She
admired the blossoming plants and trees as she
walked through the city to the beach. There were
yellow daffodils and primrose. The purple osier trees
were coming to life with small buds sitting on their
branches. The white flowers of both the Cherry Plum
and the short English Hawthorne trees fluttered in
the breeze. She couldn't resist stopping to touch the
soft, fuzzy "pussie willow" buds or to take in the
sweet, coconut aroma of the bright yellow flowers on
the Common Gorse shrubs she passed.*

*Euphemia scanned the open areas for butterflies and
bumblebees looking for their favorite plant and hers,
Ragged Robin. She knew it was silly but every year
she joined in the excitement with the other girls in
her group in an ancient Scottish custom. They put a
few Ragged Robin plants in their apron pockets and
named each plant the name of a local boy. The first
plant to bloom foretold the name of the boy the girl
would marry.*

*The problem was every year all Euphemia's plants
died before any flowers opened. It took weeks for her
friends to convince her she wouldn't be an old maid.
She didn't see any insects swarming plants; it would
be a few more weeks before the ritual could begin.*

*She spent the afternoon strolling along the beach
breathing in the fresh sea air. She watched white-
tailed sea eagles swoop and soar grabbing their
meals from the surf, enjoying her solitude until she
saw a course-looking stranger coming her way.*

*Frightened, her hands turned clammy. She thought
about running home but knew out running him would
be unlikely. No other means of escape came to mind.
She thought if she passed without looking directly at
him, she wouldn't encourage any conversation he
might have planned.*
*Dressed in a seaman's rough garb, he was unshaven,
his unwashed hair brushed his shoulders.*

She shivered.

*She turned her face toward the sea and lifted her eyes
scanning the sky to give him the message of her
disinterest. But the closer he came to her the more
she couldn't keep her eyes diverted. He had appeared
hard and stern, but suddenly she saw his features
shift into a soft, sincere smile. Their eyes locked.
Neither glanced in any other direction.*

*The young woman thought the grippe had seized her.
Unfamiliar sensations engulfed her stomach. A
burning flush claimed her face. Her heartbeat so fast
she couldn't catch her breath. She gulped, trying to
fill her lungs with air. Then her knees gave way.*

She swooned.

*The stranger moved quickly and swept her up before
she fell to the sand. With one arm under her knees
and the other bracing her upper back he began
walking toward town. But he had only taken a few
short steps when Euphemia revived, blushing with
embarrassment to find herself in his arms. She
shrieked, "Put me down at once."*

He immediately dropped his arm from under her knees. Her feet hit the ground hard. He smiled as he watched her untwist and smooth down her disheveled skirt and adjust her hat.

The stranger wanted to accompany her to her home, but she insisted she didn't need his help. She marched away from him as fast as she could with her shoes sinking in the sand. Keeping her eyes focused straight ahead of her, she hoped he would go away, but he followed behind at a slower pace.

"You might be ill." he said.

When James' father told the story he always included the fact that as the man walked, a confident smile planted itself on his unshaven face because he was sure it was the closeness to him that caused her faint.

That evening at the social, Euphemia danced with all the town's young men. She had her choice of them. No other young lady could compete with her beauty and charm. However, whenever the door opened, she turned to see if it might be the stranger entering. Some sailors attended the local socials when they were docked in the harbor. But each time she met disappointment.

Sunday it rained, dismal and cold. During the church service Euphemia wondered about her sensations before she fainted. She'd heard older girls talking about feeling 'butterflies' when a handsome young man entered a room. What she'd felt seemed more than a few flutters.

At home that afternoon Euphemia tried to read but couldn't understand the words on the page. She ran her fingers over the piano keys but didn't have the interest to play. Her parents worried that she might be coming down with a fever. She listened to their concern and retired upstairs to her bedroom. She spent the rest of the afternoon scanning the beach from her window, wondering if she would ever see the seaman again.

James had heard that story his entire life. The seaman signed onto a local fishing boat and when he returned to Montrose with money in his pocket, he walked to the beach sure she would be there waiting for him. His parents, Euphemia and Alek, married as soon as the church allowed. His mother's version always ended with ". . . and they lived happily ever after."

Only now did James understand their stirring love story. And, yes, he respected Sarah. She stood firm in her beliefs, worked hard, and helped her family. He liked the way she cared for her young sisters.

Yes, James decided, I do want a loving wife, children, and a home of my own. I love Sarah and want to share my life with her.

Decision made. His body relaxed. His eyes closed and he fell into a sound sleep.

The following Sunday James built up his courage by remembering the loving home where he grew up. It took him all day, but finally that evening he eagerly walked to the Brinkerhoff cabin.

James hadn't visited the Brinkerhoff's for a few weeks. The family missed his entertaining ways but found their own Sunday diversions. Sarah didn't expect to see him again, but then he showed up and asked her father to walk with him. She wondered what that could mean. She watched from a cabin window.

James stood straight, held his head high, and took a deep breath then used hand signs and mimes to express his intentions to Mr. Brinkerhoff. Sarah didn't understand, but it seemed despite James' clumsy presentation, her father did. He shook his head up and down as he pumped James' hand in a solid handshake while patting his back with the other hand. He led James into the cabin and announced to the entire family that James would be courting Sarah.

"*Maar, Vader, Ik ben deloofde naar*. But, Father, I am promised to Wilhelm," Sarah, cried and ran out the back door.

Her father watched in amazement as everyone in the room fell silent staring at James, his head bent, shoulders drooping. He walked out the door and away from the cabin.

Mouth opened, eyes wide, Brinkerhoff stared into the distance beyond the cabin's interior. What had he done? He thought James would make a good husband for his eldest daughter. He was pleasant, respectful, and steady. It was obvious that James cared for Sarah, and he thought Sarah liked him. *Wilhelm. Humph, where is he? If he wants to marry Sarah, he should be here.*

Sarah waited until her siblings were asleep in the loft they shared before she tiptoed back into the cabin and climbed the ladder into the loft. She threw herself onto her straw-filled ticking and buried her face in her thin pillow to muffle her sobs. How could her father give James permission to court her? She was promised to Wilhelm and Wilhelm would be in America soon. Once she stopped crying, she heard her parents.

Jan shouted at his wife, "Mother, what is wrong?" and sat heavily onto his chair at the hearth.

Speaking in a soft voice as she crossed the room to him, his wife answered, "Papa, you don't have to shout. You'll wake the children. Here, light your pipe and relax. Don't get yourself over excited." On her way to the bedroom she handed his pipe and tobacco-bag to him, then lit a stick from the fire so he could finish the soothing routine of preparing his smoke.

Mr. Brinkerhoff took a deep inhale of fresh tobacco smoke as he leaned back into the chair. His shoulders relaxed and he picked up the family Bible. When confused, he looked to the Bible for answers. Randomly opening the book, he looked down and saw *Children, obey your parents in all things, for this is well pleasing unto the Lord.* Colossians 3:20

Yes, he thought, Sarah needs to obey me. James will make a good husband for her and Wilhelm is still in The Netherlands. Again, he looked at the book in his lap and read,

Fathers, provoke not your children to anger, lest they be discouraged. Colossians 3:21

"But, God," he prayed, "how can I get her to obey me without provoking her to anger? I don't want to discourage her or cause a rift between us." With a heavy heart and no answers, Jan stared into the fire and smoked his pipe long into the night.

In the silence Sarah fretted, what will James think of me? I like him, but Wilhelm is the kind of man I want to marry.

She turned over facing the rafters in the roof. Sarah had imagined a serious life of Bible study, family prayers, and church meetings. With Wilhelm that would be assured. He shared her beliefs and religious habits. James didn't go to church and probably didn't pray or read the Bible. He was lighthearted, always joking and singing. James didn't resemble Wilhelm in any way. It didn't matter, she'd probably never see James again and Wilhelm would soon arrive. Her mind settled into sleep.

■■■

October 1687

For weeks James worked late into the night trying to forget his humiliating rejection. *What did I do wrong?* Nothing made sense to him. He had followed Mudie's suggestions. He thought Sarah cared for him as he did for her. He couldn't smile, eat, or sleep. He spoke only when spoken to and then only the few words it took to convey a somewhat satisfying answer.

Sarah went to the docks every day. She checked in with the Harbor Master to inquire what ships were due to arrive. After several days, the clerk, a young man her age, recognized her and gave her the information before she could open her mouth to ask. Laughing with him, she accepted his invitation to share his tea and biscuits.

To her surprise, one day he greeted her with scarlet cheeks as he thrust a handful of sun flowers at her. She blushed as she accepted the gift. Neither of them could make eye contact. The easiness Sarah had had with him disappeared in an instant. *What do the flowers mean? Does he want to court me, too? He knows I'm waiting for Wilhelm's ship. What do I say?*

"Thank you. They're beautiful."

He whispered so low she almost didn't hear him. "Not as beautiful as you."

Back to business, Sarah asked, "What ships are coming in today? Is Wilhelm's ship expected?"

The clerk stammered as he studied his scuffed shoes, "Not today, but within the week it should be here."

Without thinking Sarah pushed the flowers back at the clerk as she whispered, "Oh, that's wonderful." Rushing toward the door, "I must go prepare." She opened the door, turned to see the stunned look on his face, and crooned, "Thank you for the wonderful news." Leaving the door to close on its own, she hurried home to share the news.

Knowing Wilhelm would arrive soon, Sarah made peace with her father, "Papa, I love you. And I love Wilhelm. Maybe you forgot that with James coming so often. Let us forget the past and just look ahead."

"That is fine with me. I've not been happy with a rift between us."

Sarah cleaned the cabin, scrubbed her clothing, bathed, and washed her hair. She wanted everything to be perfect when Wilhelm arrived. She helped her mother pick vegetables from the kitchen garden and prepare the chicken her father slaughtered for the occasion. Hans went to the dock to meet the ship and bring Wilhelm to their home.

Waiting, Sarah paced the width of the kitchen until her father couldn't stand watching her any longer and sent her out to the yard. The table was set with their best, the meal was hot and ready to serve, and the children were clean and presentable. Sarah had reminded them to use good manners to greet Wilhelm and during their meal.

By the time Hans approached the cabin with Wilhelm, Sarah was beside herself, wringing her hands and checking her hair. Then she saw him, her Wilhelm, straight and tall. He looked weary after his voyage. He would need time to recover before she showed him around the city and countryside.

"Welcome to America" she said as she extended her hand to him.

He stumbled, not yet having his equilibrium after being at sea for many weeks. Hans caught his elbow to help steady him. Wilhelm leaned toward Hans as they walked into the cabin. Without speaking, Hans delivered Wilhelm to a seat at the table.

Wilhelm looked lost as if he didn't recognize not only the cabin but the people in it, even Sarah. Had they been apart too long? Where was the Wilhelm who wrote the letters declaring his intentions and concern for her? Why weren't they eager to be in each other's arms?

Mrs. Brinkerhoff came to the rescue with a hot cup of strong sweet-tea. Wilhelm perked up as he sipped the steaming brew. He wolfed down the food. He must not have had enough food to eat on the voyage. He didn't speak until he sat with Mr. Brinkerhoff, both enjoying their pipes.

"There were days I thought I would not survive. The storms were severe, sickness ravished the crew and passengers. I thought I was doomed to a watery grave. But, at last, God's plan has brought me to America and my dear Sarah." He smiled at her as he said the latter.

Sarah smiled in return, a shy smile she gave to strangers. *Maybe tomorrow will be better.*

Wilhelm settled in a room at Mrs. Brown's Boarding House on Westminster Street. A week passed, and then two, but he never spoke of marriage. Then without notice, he announced that he had come to know his calling. "Together with Sarah, as my wife, I will go into the wilderness and teach the word of God to the Indians." This surprised the entire Brinkerhoff family, especially Sarah.

Sarah spent many hours, day and night, questioning her feelings. She was sure she loved Wilhelm and wanted to marry him, but . . . but, what? What was missing? He seemed the same, the Wilhelm she had left in Holland, serious, pious, dedicated, and determined to do God's will.

What more could I want?

To quell her unrest, she decided to try her father's system and picked up the family Bible. She closed her eyes, opened the book, bent her face to the pages, opened her eyes and read, *Live joyfully with the wife whom thou lovest all the days of thy life . . . which he hath given thee under the sun . . . for that is thy portion in this life.* Ecclesiastes 9:9

She put the Bible back in its place. The stuffy cabin was suffocating. Needing fresh air, she left the cabin. But even in the brisk air and moonlight she could not control her thoughts. *Live joyfully?* Sarah had never heard those words spoken by clergy or her parents. *God wants me to live joyfully?* Joyfulness had never entered her mind or her thoughts of the future. Her duty was to obey her father, attend church, and obey God. She understood duty, joy was unfamiliar.

She walked away from the cabin onto the path leading to Perth Amboy. Ascertaining no one nearby, she paced back and forth along the Brinkerhoff property line talking to herself, "Wilhelm's ready to marry me and take me into the wilderness to teach the Indians. James wants to court me to test our union before we marry. A missionary's wife in the wilderness? Or maybe a blacksmith's wife in the city, near my family?"

Chilled without a shawl, she hugged herself for warmth as she worried, *How can I make such a decision?* Then looking to the heavens, she asked, "But what of love and assurances?"

Finding no answers in the stars she continued fretting, "I know Wilhelm cares for me, and marriage is assured. I think James favors me now, but what if after courting he changes his mind and doesn't want to marry me. This is a heavy choice I'm forced to make."

Startled by a sound in the forest, Sarah searched her surroundings as best she could. There were dangerous animals out and about late at night. The thought made her shudder as she headed toward the cabin, continuing her monologue.

"There's always been safety in Wilhelm's duty. James' lack of religion scares me. But, now with Wilhelm there is something missing. When I'm with James I experience a sensation strange to me. Is that the joy the scriptures are talking about? She had never questioned her father's wisdom until the night he announced James' courtship.

Walking back into the cabin, she questioned her reaction. Did her father understand something she did not?

Bereft, James longed to be in Sarah's presence, but he couldn't bring himself to return to the Brinkerhoff cabin. He couldn't face the humiliation of rejection again. Bad enough he replayed the scene over and over in his mind. His trousers hung on his hips. Mudie kept asking if he were ill.

"No, sir, just not hungry."

He wished Will hadn't left Perth Amboy. He'd know what to do to rid James of this constant heartache.

Whenever James heard a warbler's song or saw black-eyed Susans, Sarah's favorite wildflower, he wanted to share them with her. In his dreams he saw himself holding her in his arms, kissing her, feeling her heart beating against his chest. He would wake in tears and sweat asking himself, *What should I do?*

...

Sarah could've been hanging on tenterhooks. Any sudden noise or movement caused her to gasp and startle. Her pleasant disposition disappeared replaced with quick critical comments, eye rolling and nose wrinkling.

Her father sulked around the house unsure of his daughter's sentiments toward him. He asked his wife, "Is Sarah angry with me again? I don't understand. Wilhelm's here now, she should be happy."

Frustrated with her husband's lack of understanding Lijsbeth walked away from her spinning wheel to where he sat by the hearth and tried to explain in a way a man might understand, "Jan, I believe Sarah's angrier with herself than she is with anyone and especially you."

"Herself? Humph, she sure doesn't act like it."

"Sarah is a God-fearing dutiful woman. She promised herself to Wilhelm because he is a pious man. She'd never met a man like James. He's full of laughter and song. We protected Sarah within our strong reformed community. Here, in this new world, she's meeting people with different beliefs and customs."

"Is that bad? Should I have kept our family in Haarlem?"

Reaching her husband, Lijsbeth placed her hand on his shoulder, "No, Jan, you did what you thought was right. We followed because we trust and love you. But Sarah wasn't prepared." Kneeling at his side she continued, "It's been an adjustment for all of us, but more so for Sarah. She thought her life would follow her plan, but when James came along, she experienced emotions she didn't know existed."

Scratching his balding head, Jan asked, "Emotions? What are you talking about?"

"She knows obedience and duty with Wilhelm. James brought her love and happiness. I expect she just hasn't figured out how to have all four, obedience & duty to God as well as love and happiness with a man."

Jan held his wife's hand in his and looked into her loving eyes, "So, what must I do?"

"Be patient. Love her. Pray for her. Be assured she loves her father as strongly as she ever has." Lijsbeth kissed her husband's forehead and returned to her spinning.

Jan puffed his pipe in contemplation.

...

Wilhelm stayed away. He said he had to prepare for his Indian Ministry, but, in fact, he hid. He was discomfited around Sarah's uneasy spirit. He needed her to be firm in her duty as his helpmate. Morning, noon, and night he repeated the same prayer, "Oh, God, please show Sarah thy plan for her."

Families

Then one day Emily presented Sarah with a bouquet of wild blue Phlox, "These are for you, so you'll be happy again."

Sarah's eyes widened as she took in a quick breath, "What do you mean . . . happy . . . again? I am happy. Wilhelm is here and we'll be married soon. That's what I've always wanted."

Without hesitation Emily blurted, "You don't look happy. And you're . . . cranky . . . a lot."

"Cranky?"

Emily looked into her oldest sister's dark eyes and whispered, "I want you to be happy again, like you were when James came here."

Unexpected tears ran down Sarah's cheeks as she hugged Emily to her. "My sweet Emily. I am so sorry, and I promise I won't be cranky anymore." Sarah turned Emily loose. "Now go play."

Smelling the sweet aroma of the flowers as she placed stems in a jar of water Sarah pondered Emily's innocent words. *Happy like when James came here. H-m-m-m-m.*

Sarah grabbed her bonnet and shawl and almost sang, "Mama, I have errands." Then she walked out the cabin door.

Lijsbeth stared at the sudden change in her daughter and hoped she had come to a decision. The right decision for her.

...

First stop, Mrs. Brown's Boarding House to speak with Wilhelm.

Surprised to see her at midday, he showed nervousness in his furrowed brow. "Sarah? I wasn't expecting you, but come in. At least for a moment."

Sarah stepped into the parlor, furnished in dark reds and browns. Hardly any light penetrated the heavy velvet draperies. She shivered though the room wasn't cold. He offered her a chair and cup of tea. She refused both. He paced the width of the parlor unable to look at her. She seemed different. In fact, he'd never seen her so animated and bright eyed.

"Wilhelm, please stand still so I can talk to you."

He stopped mid-stride, almost losing his balance, then dropped onto the settee.

Sarah sat next to him and took his hands in hers. "I know it's expected that we marry, but you need a woman devoted to you and your ministry, and that's just not me. Not anymore. Please forgive me."

Wilhelm leaned back away from Sarah. Then, with his lips pressed tight together, he looked away and down at the well-worn carpet under his feet. Frowning, he continued, "What changed your mind? What, pray tell, did I do to lose your devotion?"

Sarah looked at their entwined hands and shook her head. This was more difficult than she had imagined. "Nothing.

You're the same Wilhelm I imaged I'd live my life with. It's me who changed." After clearing her throat, she continued, "I feel God has a different path for me. I found my way in the scriptures. It took me the past few weeks to understand completely, but now that I do, I must act on His prompting." She looked into his eyes beseeching his forgiveness.

"Forgive you? Of course, that is God's command. We are to forgive others." Looking Heaven-ward Wilhelm's shoulders relaxed. Smiling, he patted her hands. Then he stood, lifting her hands to ease her to her feet, and walked her to the door. "I understand. You must follow God's plan for you as I will His plan for me. Thank you for releasing me from our promise. Now I go to the savages unencumbered." He held her hands in his and pressed them to his heart. "Farewell, Sarah."

Nodding her head toward him she whispered, "Wilhelm," and left.

Earlier when she'd stood on the stoop knocking on the boarding house door, she had carried a heavy burden. Walking out, back into the sunlight, she smiled and caught herself humming a tune.

Greeting passers-by with a happy smile she practically skipped along the wooden walkway up Westminster Street then along High Street toward the Blacksmith Shop. But the closer she got the wilder the flutters in her stomach. She clutched her midriff and hid behind a wide old oak tree where she could see the forge but go unnoticed by anyone there. She watched as a customer tipped his hat to James and walked away.

She stared as James wiped his forehead with a grimy kerchief. She'd never seen him at work, only in the country on his days off. Today she thought he looked unwell, thinner than she remembered, with no energy in his step or glimmer in his eyes.

She froze, ignoring the chirping birds hopping in the branches above her. She wondered if she should approach. Then remembering Emily's innocent face and her wish for Sarah's happiness, Sarah, on wobbling knees, stepped out from behind the tree and walked directly to James.

···

Concentrating on shaping a lump of red-hot iron into a horseshoe, James didn't notice her until he plunged the iron in the slack tub and heard a feminine squeal as steam filled the air around him. *Am I delirious seeing Sarah in the steam?* Her voice jolted him back to reality. She stood in front of him, not an illusion. He looked at his soot-covered hands and stammered, "S-sarah?"

"Hello, James. How are you?"

Working hard to stand tall and not shuffle his feet he answered, "Fine. I'm fine. Well enough. And you?"

Her answer found its way through a radiant smile, "Oh, I've never been better."

She looked pleased with herself. He figured she was here to announce her marriage. He asked, "What brings you to the blacksmith? Do you have an order to place?"

"No, no. I need to talk to you. Are you too busy now?"

James walked to the bucket of drinking water and gulped from the dipper. Then wiping his chin with the back of his hand, he nodded toward her hiding place. "Let's go sit on that bench in the shade."

"That would be nice. Thank you."

James led her to the bench and scattered dust as he attempted to clean a spot for her to sit. She thanked him beaming at his thoughtfulness.

"So, what is it you want to say?"

Sarah looked down at her folded hands.

Waiting, James' memory flipped back to the day his mother informed him of his future as a blacksmith. He feared Sarah would present an even more difficult challenge, sure he'd lost her.

Clearing her throat, Sarah began, "James, I'm not sure how to begin."

James' words spilled out faster than either of them expected as his face flushed. "That's all right. Are you here to tell me you're marrying Wilhelm and going off to convert the Indians?"

She turned and looked deep into his eyes, "No, James. I'm here to apologize."

Surprise registered in his eyes, "Apologize? For what?"

"Wait. Please, just listen." Sarah looked at her hands again, as James waited, silent. Then she straightened and faced James with resolve, "I was wrong to send you away as I did. I was confused. Your lightheartedness . . . it scared me. You don't go to church. That scares me. I've never known music, dancing, or storytelling, and all of it scares me."

"I'm sorry, Sarah—"

"James, please, let me finish." She wiped perspiration from her face with her clean, white handkerchief. "The night you left, I read the Bible for guidance and a verse spoke to me as never before. But I didn't understand. Will you forgive me?"

"Yes, of course. What did the verse say?"

Ignoring his question, Sarah continued, "Today Emily told me I'm . . . 'cranky'." A slight smile flashed then vanished into a frown.

James grinned trying to imagine Sarah cranky, "You, cranky?"

Sarah looked away, up the road at children playing. Then turning back, with a shy smile she admitted, "Yes. She's right. I've been miserable inside and out. I couldn't listen to you or my father or . . . even the Word of God . . . until today. Emily brought me to my senses."

Sarah, silent, stood and stepped away from James.

James remained sitting on the bench, elbows on his knees, forehead in his hands, eyes closed. "Now I'm the one who doesn't understand. What are you trying to say?"

Facing James, Sarah looked down at him and, almost whispering, explained, "The scripture I read that night admonishes God's people to have joy in marriage. I thought God wanted me to live a staid life. But today with Emily's help I finally understand. James, I want the joy God wants for me." Sarah shivered in a sudden cold breeze and pulled her shawl tight around her shoulders.

James looked up into Sarah's eyes, "Thank you for explaining all of this to me. I'm sure you'll find God's joy with Wilhelm."

Sitting again close to James, her left knee barely touching his right one, Sarah's soft voice sounded shaky, "No, James. I want the joy you bring to my life."

James couldn't believe what he was hearing, "But I thought—"

Placing two soft fingers on his lips, she whispered, "Sh-h-h. James, will you marry me?"

Jumping to his feet he shouted, "Absolutely! Bloody Hell, absolutely I'll marry you!"

That week James worked intensely, but with light feet and mood. He could not stop smiling. After finishing an order of nails, he heated one until it would bend and then formed it into a circle, a ring for Sarah to express his never-ending love for her.

James approached Mudie, and pushing the hair off his forehead he began, "Mr. Mudie, Sarah and I want to marry.

You mentioned that you might give me permission if I agree to stay on after my indenture contract is over."

Before he could continue Mudie jumped in, "Congratulations! Yes, I did, and I will."

"Thank you, sir."

"I've been thinking about it since we spoke last. Since you have less than a year, how would you feel about staying an extra two years? You and Sarah can live in your cabin."

James nodded, "That sounds workable."

Mudie didn't hesitate, "And, as a matter of fact, I'm in need of an assistant to help Mrs. Burnett my housekeeper. Ask Sarah if she'd be willing to take on the task. Her work could buy out your contract and then continue to cover rent on the cabin. Then I could change your contract from indenture to employee and pay you wages. Does that sound fair to you?"

James smiled and his body relaxed, "Thank you, sir. I'll talk to Sarah about your offer."

...

James and Sarah married the third day of November sixteen-eighty-seven and moved into James small cabin. Marriage fit them both. They worked well together wanting nothing more than to share their love and do their part in the community. Sarah accepted Mudie's offer to assist Mrs. Burnett.

A hard worker, Sarah soon learned the ins and outs of the Mudie household. With her arthritis Mrs. Burnett tended to remain on the main floor. She assigned Sarah to the second floor often referring to her as a "Godsend."

Mudie's daughters Elizabeth, Issy, and Janet, didn't want things to change. However, once they understood Mrs. Burnett's needs, they welcomed Sarah to their private domain.

Sarah kept their rooms immaculate, during the winter a warm fire in their hearths. She mended, brushed, and maintained their wardrobe. Margaret and Issy enjoyed teaching her the duties of a personal maid. Janet kept busy away from home, but happily joined in the lessons whenever she could. Once the girls were dressed for dinner, they excused Sarah for the day.

Sarah learned to help the girls dress and fix their hair. She learned to curtsy, stand silent until spoken to, and every other protocol that wealthy Scotts followed. The family included Sarah in their holiday traditions. Sarah learned to show polite surprise accepting a boxed gift from Mudie on the day after Christmas, Boxing Day.

The girls showed respect toward Sarah, but also teased her. They told her that someday she'd need to supervise her own servants. She listened to their instructions and with intent watched their demonstrations. She doubted she'd ever have servants, but with the training, if perchance she had daughters, she would be able to teach them skills to find work. Sarah couldn't have any greater hopes for her children then to embrace the faith her family taught her, give an honest days' work, and find a spouse to love them as James loved her. And, of course, give her grandchildren.

For Sarah, time seemed fleeting. She took pleasure in her home and time with James. She enjoyed the Mudie girls and taking her place as a married woman in the community. Once sure a babe grew in her womb she could often be heard saying, "My cup of blessings runneth over." However, James seemed worried.

After coaxing him several times, he confessed his fears, "My mother almost died the day I was born. The thought of losing you causes me to tremble. Sarah, I don't want any harm to come to you."

"Oh, James, I couldn't be happier. Please don't worry. If it be God's will both the baby and I will survive."

"I don't know if there is a God, Sarah, and if there is why did he take my parents from me?"

She hugged James tightly. Sarah didn't have an answer, but she prayed for James' concerns and for his soul. His unbelief still frightened her.

■■■

August 1688

They named their son in honor of Sarah's father. In the evenings James delighted in playing the tin whistle his father had played for him to sooth the infant. John, a quiet, happy babe made it easy for Sarah to continue her work with the Mudie's. He spent his days in a cradle by the kitchen hearth or tied into Sarah's shawl as she worked. That is, unless Janet spirited him away. Caring for him seemed to ease her longing for the Gordon children. Sarah knew being needed lessened Janet's grief.

While Sarah swept the ashes from Janet's bedroom hearth, Janet held John, bounced him in her arms, and explained how she had come to visit the Gordon's in Scotland. "My mother took an immediate fondness toward Thomas Gordon's late wife, Ellen. A young woman who Mother said, 'married at seventeen, loved her husband with all her heart, and never denied him.'

"Knowing I loved young children, even though still in my own childhood, mother often took me when she called on Ellen. While they visited, I played with the Gordon's four young children. Soon I became extremely helpful. I'd rather had been acting the nanny than learning to be a proper lady. I spent a great deal of time at the Gordon home."

Sarah emptied the small scoop of ashes into a pail. "Ellen must have appreciated your help and your companionship."

"Yes, in fact, we became dear friends. Ellen never treated me like a child. We shared confidences and I learned more about being a woman than I ever could have from my mother or my giggling, gossiping spinster sisters."

Sarah didn't want to encourage Janet in her flippant description of her family, but she giggled in spite of herself.

Staring into the empty fireplace Janet sighed, "When I heard, what my father called 'good news', I couldn't believe it. Thomas Gordon would be going to America and taking his wife and children with him."

Touching Janet's arm, Sarah nearly whispered, "Janet, it must have been difficult for you to watch them go."

"It was devastating. Father promised to come back in two years, and I determined that if he returned to New Jersey, I would be with him. I wanted nothing more than to be with Ellen and her children." Laughing she continued, "Well, as you see I got my way. I wish I could have seen Mother's face when she realized I'd left."

"Oh, my, has she forgiven you, yet?" Sarah stood and brushed ashes from her apron into the pail.

"I really don't know, and it doesn't matter. She's where she wants to be, and I'm where I want to be. Well, at least where I wanted to be. Now all I can do is help Mr. Gordon as best I know how."

"Yes, your sisters told me your scheme and how you manage to keep your service a secret. You're like a little fairy doing good for a parted friend. I'm sure Ellen still appreciates what you do for her."

■■■

"Poor Janet," Sarah whispered as she snuggled closer to James.

He reached out and wrapped her in his arms as she pulled their marriage quilt tight around them. "Why do you say that?"

"You know Thomas Gordon's wife and six children all passed away. Janet helped tend the babes and became a dear friend of their mother. She said she didn't want them to leave Scotland."

"Oh, that explains her sad eyes the day we sailed. I wasn't aware of her strong connection to the Gordons."

Looking up at James face, "You knew the Mudies in Scotland?"

"Yes, Janet's older sister Jean and I were childhood friends. In fact, I thought I might wed her." Nuzzling Sarah's neck he continued, "But I didn't understand love back then . . . before you." Chuckling James went on, "When I was young, I thought mother and father were droll as they looked into each other's eyes as if they were seeing a sweet cake they wanted to sample instead of seeing another person. Mother would say, "The Sea enriches." And father, a seaman who she met on the beach, would take her face in his rough hands and whisper, "The rose adorns." I remember my discomfort.

"But once I matured, I realized they were reciting the Montrose motto. I still didn't understand that kind of love. Until now." James kissed Sarah with the passion he was explaining.

"M-m-m-m." Sarah purred and furrowed deeper into his arms.

"But as it turned out, Jean deserted me with the rest of my friends when my mother lowered my social standing by sending me to be a blacksmith's apprentice."

She reached up and stroked his cheek, "I'm sorry. That must have been difficult."

"Looking back, it was for the best and I got me Will, a good mate. I didn't need a woman back then."

"As young as Janet is, she's working through her grief by secretly helping Mr. Gordon. She goes to his house everyday while he's away. She tidies up the house and helps the cook with whatever chores are needed that day. She weeds and waters Mrs. Gordon's garden. Late in the afternoon she sets the dinner table and puts out fresh flowers when they're available. Then before she leaves, she places Mr. Gordon's books and pipes on the table next to his armchair."

"That's quite a lot for a young girl."

"But that's not all." Sarah sat up so she could see James' face. "She enlisted her father to invite Mr. Gordon to Sunday dinners with their family so he wouldn't have to fend for himself on his cook's day off."

"Sounds like she's overly thoughtful for her age."

"Yes, she's beyond her years in her care for those she loves. But at times she's a normal child and flippant with her sisters. Today she referred to them as 'giggling, gossiping spinsters.'" Sarah couldn't help giggling again.

A quick chuckle rattled in James' throat, "Is she right? Are they?" He wiggled down under the quilt and put his head on the feather pillow Sarah had stuffed for him.

After she rested her head on his chest, he circled her with his strong arms. She answered, "At times, yes. They're like their father, independent and determined to have their way. But they're still young. I'm not sure they'll find husbands here where society is so different from what they're used to."

James' embrace slackened and Sarah heard his soft even breathing. With a smile, she closed her eyes and joined him in sleep.

...

November third marked the first anniversary of James and Sarah's marriage. Sarah's work as Mrs. Burnett's assistant had paid off James' indenture contract and next month's wages would go toward rent on their cabin. James, now an employee, more than compensated Mudie for the contract termination. Mudie released James from any obligations to him. James was free to work anywhere, but his loyalty to the man that gave him his happy life kept James in Mudie's employ.

It seemed to Sarah, just as she became used to caring for John another babe came along. Sixteen months later, December sixteen-eighty-nine, Young James burst into the world howling, rambunctious from the start. He demanded attention, but between the Mudie sisters and Sarah they managed. Mrs. Burnett moved a rocking chair closer to the hearth insisting on time to cuddle each baby.

...

Sarah's day began as any other. On her feet before daylight, she prepared breakfast for her and James then fed the boys. After cleaning up she dressed her sons and walked to the Mudie house. As usual she settled the infants and gathered cleaning supplies, then climbed the stairs to Margaret's room. The sisters, instead of their usual morning solemnity bustled around the room pulling dresses out of the wardrobe and babbling about the attributes of each.

Margaret welcomed her with a sing-song greeting, "Good morning, Sarah. 'Tis a lovely day."

"I'tis that. Are you packing for a trip?"

"Oh, no. We're not taking a trip. We're having guests for dinner. Father has invited a wealthy young Scotsman to join us this evening."

Issy joined in, "And we have to look our best. He's unmarried and traveling without family or friend. Father said we need to make him feel welcome and happy to be in America."

Sarah smiled knowingly, "Yes, you do and I'm sure you will. What can I do to help?" She chuckled inside not used to seeing these young women in a frivolous dither.

■■■

All the rest of that week Sarah watched Margaret cater to the young man's needs, flirt, and coax him into distracting activities. *She is certainly taking her part seriously.* Sarah smiled to herself.

Later in the month while helping the girls prepare for a party Sarah heard Margaret lament, "I wish we could announce our engagement tonight, but Papa says that's not proper until we have his father's blessing."

"That's the way it's done in Scotland." Issy said as she sighed.

"Well, this will be a wonderful evening to wish him God's speed in his return to me. I love him so. I don't know how I will stand spending even one day without him."

Impatient, as always, Issy said, "Oh, I'm sure you'll manage."

Sounding more like a spoiled child than a soon-to-be betrothed lady, Margaret shot back at her sister, "You're jealous. I can't help it that Horace chose me over you. He just did."

"All right, girls, where did you put your hair ribbons?" Sarah asked to get the subject changed into a friendlier direction.

...

At the dock the following day, Margaret waved farewell to her promised, then went home and began planning her marriage celebration. Issy tried to talk her into waiting until Horace returned, but Margaret wouldn't hear of it. Their father didn't interfere. As the weeks went by, Sarah watched and listened as Margaret became giddier and more excited, and Issy transformed into a quarrelsome counterpart. Tension between the two heightened every day igniting emotional outbursts from both.

Several months of discontent in Mudie's household came to an end when he gathered his daughters and relayed the news with as much gentleness as he could. Word had come that the ship Horace had sailed on had not reached Scotland. The crew and all passengers were assumed dead by drowning or pirates. But of course, Margaret could not bear to hear it.

Margaret never stopped waiting for her Horace to return. Issy walked her to the docks nearly every day where they would watch passengers disembark, Margaret always expecting Horace to run to her and take her in his arms. Issy faithfully walked her broken-hearted sister back home. Evenings Margaret paced from room to room or wrote long letters asking when he'd return.

As Margaret escaped into her fantasy world, Issy became more patient, caring for her beloved sister. Issy gave up any hope that she might have had for her own family, tying her future to her sister's happiness.

There were days Margaret would imagine Horace had arrived and she would reenact his proposal. She'd sip Champaign and smile as the family congratulated her on her good fortune. On other days Issy managed to get Margaret out to sit in the sun while she read one of Father's treasured volumes, no longer contradicting Margaret's belief that Horace would return some day. The entire family colluded in Margaret's denial of the loss of Horace and soon she and her ever-vigilant protector, Issy, became recluses. The two forever waited the return of a ghost.

After several weeks of the charade Janet could no longer hold back her disagreement with the situation. She sat down with Issy and her father, "I think Margaret should return to Mother. We can't do anything to help her here. Maybe mother's attention would break through her delusions. Or a doctor there could help." No doctor in New Jersey had been able to break Margaret from her spell.

Issy protested, "Just because you've gotten over Ellen's death, doesn't mean Margaret will ever recover from her loss. After all, you're just a child. You don't know love between a man and a woman."

To counteract Issy's near hysteria, Janet whispered, "I might not know about love, but I know it's not right to encourage Margaret's imaginings. Horace will never return. Giving up life over her loss is not romantic, it's a sickness."

"Oh, you know that do you? You're a doctor now?"

"No, I'm not a doctor, but the way Margaret lives is not natural. Father, can't you see? She needs help, and she's not getting it here."

Neither Issy nor her father listened to Janet's concerns. They didn't want to upset Margaret any more than necessary. So, the years passed by with no change for the Mudies.

Thomas and John Gordon's letters shared concerns and hopes for the future of New Jersey.

November 1690

Dearest Thomas,

I am saddened to learn of Governor Barclay's death, I am afraid the Proprietors Group cannot agree on a new appointee. There seems no end to

*the anger and animosity within the group. I don't
know what will come of this.*

*Until we work together and agree on a candidate,
East New Jersey will have no governor to lead its
progress. I pray lawlessness will not overtake the
province. Please do whatever is necessary to
protect yourself.*

*How will we recover our investment if settlers will
not pay their rents and no one in the colony will
enforce our demands? I'm afraid this experiment
will not succeed if this continues. You may have to
return to Scotland and leave America to the Natives
and the Dutch.*

*I pray your endeavors are worth the efforts you put
forth. May God bless you through these times of
unrest.*

Yours — John

January 1691

Dear John,

*I understand your concern and negative view of our
task. However, if you were here, you'd see that this
land is worth fighting for. I'll not surrender. This
life is difficult. Indeed, I've lost my beloved wife
and six children. They are now a part of this New
World. But I made a pledge to God that their deaths
would not be in vain.*

*Whether I ever love again or enjoy the felicity of
home fires, I will remain here. I'll use my
knowledge and what authority I may have to make
East New Jersey a place of fairness and freedom.*

103

*This is truly a garden spot and will support many
plantations, craftsmen, settlements, and families. I
am honored to play a part in this grand enterprise.
I pray that the proprietors will be able to agree on
an ethical appointee to lead this government.*

Yours — Thomas

Then in March, Thomas received, amongst news from
Montrose, an acknowledgement from his brother,

*Please forgive the pessimism of my last epistle. I
know your duty there is difficult. If I cannot
understand your commitment, I do appreciate it.*

Gordon did his best to collect rents, and at times met with
success. He represented his brother's interest in court
whenever occasion arose. Gordon created a circle of
relationships with men he admired for their convictions and
honesty. His determination to be part of New Jersey's future
helped distract him from the grief since the death of his wife
and children. He worked long days so as not to be in his empty
house. Janet Mudie continued to help his cook maintain and
improve his home and he appreciated her efforts. But in the
silence, he missed his wife and children.

While the Mudie family's routines remained a dull reminder
of loss, a hot muggy August day in sixteen-ninety-one brought
Alexander, named after James' father, and brought more joy
into the Fitchett home. His wide eyes expressed as much
wonder with the world around him as his name sakes had.

They nicknamed him Sany and watched him thrive. Whenever Mrs. Burnett finished her chores, she told the boys stories. All three vied to be the special one who sat on her ample lap. And, of course, Janet found time to play governess. Sarah didn't know how she could be any happier with life.

The following year Gordon received news from his brother informing him of the proprietor's decision.

March 1692

Thomas,

There has been a change you'll be pleased to hear. The Proprietors' Group, at least many of us, approved a Scot, Andrew Hamilton, as Governor. He will sail for Perth Amboy soon.

Please make accommodations ready for his comfort on arrival.

Thanking you in advance — John

A few months after Andrew Hamilton's arrival, Thomas Gordon again sat in Mudie's study after the family's Sunday evening meal of roast duck and custard pudding. Joining his host in their usual mug of ale, Gordon asked, "Well, Mudie, what do you think of our new Governor?"

"Hamilton seems to be fit. Rent payments haven't improved, but there's less contention in the land."

"Yes, I believe Hamilton will lead us into success. I've accepted an appointment from him to sit as Clerk of the Court of Common Right. I should be able to quell perspective disturbances in court."

Walking toward the sitting room to join her sisters, nineteen-year-old Janet heard the men's louder than normal voices. She noticed the study door ajar and grabbed the knob to close it when she heard her father laugh out loud then say, "I hope so. I'm too old to take up arms."

Impetuous as always, instead of closing the door, Janet pushed it wide open and rushed into the room exclaiming, "Father, are we going to war?"

Both men stared in silence, giving Janet a moment to control her thoughts. Blushing, she examined her shoes before speaking again. "Father, please forgive me. I shouldn't have burst into your study. I only stopped at the door to pull it closed, but when I heard you speak of war, a fright possessed me."

"Well, now that you're here, do come in and sit." He pointed to a straight-backed wooden chair. "No, child, there is no war on the horizon. You have no need for worry on that point. Gordon and I were discussing how to get tenants to pay their rents. Have you any suggestions?"

"I don't, but why don't the Proprietors just sell the land to the settlers like you do? Surely, they would profit from their investment, too."

Gordon joined the conversation, "Well, Miss Janet, you are correct. They would make a profit once, as your father and I do, buying and selling land. But the proprietors' intent is to

106

own the plantations and benefit every year when crops are sold."

Thinking through the explanation, she spoke slowly, "So, . . . they lease their land to the farmers, . . . share the profits . . . and want a rent besides?"

"Precisely. That's the way it's been done for centuries back home."

Janet began timidly, "But . . . Mr. Gordon, we're not back home." Then sounding surer of her reasoning, she continued, "We're in a new land where people have come to have freedoms they couldn't have before." Looking into his eyes she couldn't tell if he meant to tease her, but unblinking, she finished with a strong statement, "I can see why they might not want to pay the rents to absentee landlords."

Mudie broke in, "Janet, are you siding with the rebels?" Laughing again, and then emptying his mug, he chided, "Don't let anyone outside this house hear you talk like that."

Speaking fast as she stood, she said, "Yes, sir. I mean no, sir, I won't." and rushed from the room pulling the door shut. Her ear to the door Janet heard Gordon's voice.

"Well, Mudie, your wee lass moves like a sprite and she does speak her mind."

And her father's reply, "Aye, she's nimble all right and says what she thinks, sometimes without thinking first. She always has, and I expect always will."

For the next two years, Thomas Gordon fulfilled his assignment as Clerk of the Court of Common Right. Mudie continued to oversee his gristmill, blacksmith forge, and South River plantation. As the capital of East New Jersey, Perth Amboy welcomed more settlers and became a bustling community.

Sweet Potatoes & Friendship

September 1694

On market day in Perth Amboy, farmers came from one to two days' journey away to sell their goods. They offered flour, potatoes, tomatoes, corn, beef, pork, chicken, eggs, milk, and cheese. The city dwellers didn't keep their own animals or large gardens. Most had kitchen gardens where they grew small plants like carrots, beans, onions, and peas and purchased other items from farms outside the city.

Anytime a ship docked, imported goods were available—tea, coffee, sugar and spices, cotton, and on rare occasions, silk. Sometimes there were luxury items from foreign ports, bracelets, fabrics, and sweet treats. The Lenape Indians brought soft leather moccasins, bags, belts, and capes beautifully decorated with their expert hand-crafted beadwork.

Sarah saw market day as a joyful adventure. She always wore her best day-dress, made from the blue broadcloth her father had woven for her and pinned a bluebird's feather to her bonnet. She smiled brightly as she made her way around the selling carts. She loved hearing the chatter of the people, accents, and languages from all over the world. There were English, German, French, Dutch, Italian, Chinese, and several native tribal languages.

109

If a slave ship had arrived there'd be indistinguishable murmuring from Africans chained together on the dock. Sarah didn't understand the words, but she knew they were pleading for their freedom, to be returned to their homes and families.

The Netherlands had a long slave trade history and church leaders said Africans had no souls. Sarah's parents never discussed slavery with her, and she never brought up the subject. She wanted to be loyal to her country and her faith, but deep in her heart she knew it was wrong. The slaves were the only part of market days that Sarah hated. She always said a silent prayer for them and their families.

One cool day in early autumn, Sarah saw a Negro woman at a selling cart. A slave selling anything at the market was unheard of. No one trusted slaves with their goods or their money. She watched curiously as the woman tried to sell her wares, orange-red, potato-like objects in strange shapes and sizes. Sarah noticed that most potential shoppers shook their heads and walked away.

Sarah kept her eyes on the strange looking items as she tentatively approached the cart. The Negro woman smiled and pointing at the strange items explained in The King's English mixed with a Scottish lilt and a slow slurry drawl, "These sweet potatoes."

Startled from her imaginings Sarah asked, "Sweet potatoes? I've never seen these before. Where did they come from?"

"My husband and I grow 'em. He worked the fields in Jamaica. We brought seedlings to New Jersey with us."

Sarah's voice wavered a little as she adjusted her bonnet and ventured, "You're from Jamaica, but aren't . . . slaves?"

Quick and firm the woman answered, "No, Ma'am, we free blacks."

Returning to the wares, Sarah smiled, "What do they taste like? Do you cook them?"

"Yes, Ma'am, you cook 'em, next to the fire an' turn 'em so they cook through, but not burn. They soft, juicy an' sweet. Very delicious," as she explained she handed one of the potatoes to her customer.

It felt rough, but Sarah noticed that her fingers could easily rub off the thin outer layer. The woman cut one of the potatoes in half and showed Sarah the orange flesh inside. She explained to Sarah how to tell when they're ready to eat. Sarah bought three. She said she'd try them and see if her family liked them. She paid the woman and walked away with her strange purchase wondering if she'd done the right thing.

When Sarah brought the sweet potatoes home the children laughed at their odd shapes. Three-year-old Sany was especially fascinated with them. He ran to a shelf and grabbed a well-worn book filled with drawings of animals and plants by Ray and Willughby. He took it to his mother and showed her how one potato looked like a seal and another, a bird.

Studying this book was Sany's favorite pastime, next to drawing that is. Mr. Mudie had given the book to the family after he noticed Sany's interest in drawing animals and flowers. The book had sketches of plants and animals from all over the world. Sany could study and draw God's creations he'd never yet seen.

Sany drew with whatever he could find, charred wood, crushed berries, and loose horsehair. He left his pictures wherever he went: in the dust, on fences, and the walls of the forge. Sarah was pleased that Sany used his imagination and was interested in the natural world around him. She encouraged his innate talents.

One of the potatoes was short and fat. One was long, thin, and curved—the seal. The third had a beak-like shape on the small round end and then curved slightly into a larger round body that blended into a thin tail—the bird. They were a yellow-orange color, no one in the family had ever seen anything like them.

Anxious about cooking the new potatoes, Sarah washed them gently and laid them on the hearth, not in the cook fire. She turned them as the woman had directed. James teased her about learning to cook Jamaican potatoes. When Sarah tested them with a fork and found them tender, a thick orange substance oozed from the holes.

Sarah put one potato on James plate, one on her plate, and split the largest between the three boys. Looking around the table she saw frightened faces staring back at her. Neither James nor the boys seemed eager to try the new food. Sarah smiled reassuringly and made a game out of their first taste.

"All right. We'll try this together. Get some of the orange on your fork and when I count to three, we'll all put the potato in our mouths." The five of them gathered a small piece of the soft flesh onto their forks. "One. Two. Three. Go." They opened their mouths and dramatically placed the pulp onto their tongues. Together they closed their mouths and tasted sweet potato for the first time. They laughed and giggled pleased with surprise of the potatoes' delicious taste. The family gobbled them up and begged Sarah to buy more. "I will if I see the woman again."

The following market day Sarah made a beeline to the black woman's selling cart, glad to see she had more sweet potatoes to sell. Sarah smiled broadly and told the woman about their tasting adventure.

Pleased, the woman laughed with Sarah as she pictured the family fearfully moving their forks from their plates to their mouths. Then leaning toward Sarah, she pointed to her heart and whispered, "My name's Nkechinyere. Say, Un-ke-chee."

Sarah complied.

"Means whatever God gives. My family calls me Kechi. You can, too."

Sarah introduced herself and Kechi asked, "What does your name Sarah mean?"

"European names rarely have meanings. My parents chose my name to honor a woman in our Bible. That Sarah stayed obedient to God's words and He blessed her in her old age. I

113

guess they hoped I would remain obedient and be rewarded." Smiling Sarah sorted through the sweet potatoes picking up a half dozen. She made sure to take odd shapes for Sany's imagination to work on.

Before Sarah stepped away, Kechi offered, "Come to my land, I'll show you how sweet potatoes grow. We give field Negros work orders in the morning. I take them a midday meal. Then evenings before the sun sets, I walk the fields, come then. Bring your children. I have two daughters, Acuchi, wealth from God, and Udo, peace. They'll be with me."

James voiced uneasiness about Sarah's plans, but gave in to her wishes as he did more often than not. After supper James returned to the forge while Sarah and the children began their adventure. John hitched Lulu, their pony, to their small wooden cart. Lulu, white with brown splotches, what the Indians called a pinto, was small, gentle, and cooperative, perfect for the family.

Sarah followed Kechi's directions and had no problem finding her fields. Kechi's two young daughters waved as they approached. While Kechi showed Sarah the plants, John and James roamed through wild growth surrounding the planted field chasing toads and squirrels. Kechi's daughters played house using Sany as their living doll.

After a short walk by the sweet potato fields, Kechi invited Sarah into her cabin for tea. Sarah could tell the cabin was made well. No drafts would blow through the frame.

Furnishings made by craftsmen from local material showed family use. Curtains, cushions, and blankets of vivid greens, yellows, and reds raised her spirits. She was expecting dark sparse living quarters like most of her neighbors had, but here books, shells, and statutes decorated all corners. A delightful aroma drifted from the rafters where herbs, flowers, and spices hung drying.

Kechi served tea and biscuits from a hand-painted porcelain set. Much different from Sarah's plain red clay pot from The Netherlands. Sipping and munching the two women shared their stories of how they came to be in Perth Amboy. Sarah gave a short version of her family's move and meeting James.

Then Kechi began, "My mother is Igbo from Nigeria. Her family owns a large plantation on fertile land near thick forests. There are many tributaries that run through the land into the Great Kwa River, past a small village called Atimbo, then into the Ocean." Sarah listened with keen interest.

"Women in Nigeria manage the plantations. My mother would have, as her mother had, in a long line of Nnennes— grandmothers—before her. From the beginning of time Nnennes grew yams, round white fleshed roots that sustained the people. But when Portuguese sailors brought us sweet potatoes from across the ocean her family learned to grow the best in the land."

"So, how did you get to Perth Amboy?" Sarah wondered aloud.

"When my mother was a young girl, slave traders kidnapped her and took her to Jamaica. They sold her to a man named Gordon, a young Scot sent to the West Indies by his father to oversee a sugar plantation. He was inexperienced and lonely. He bought several slaves to work the fields and then saw my mother. She told me she felt a burning in her heart when he looked at her. He bought her as his house slave but loved her as a wife."

In her mind Sarah could hear her preacher condemning the young lovers. Trying to remove the judgmental thoughts, Sarah stared into her cup watching the tea swirl as she stirred the brown liquid.

Kechi sipped her tea and continued, "After I was born, my father's father became angry and sent a woman from Scotland to be his wife. He obeyed his father and married her, but never left my mother's heart or bed."

Blushing, Sarah exclaimed, "Oh, my! All of you lived in the same house?"

"Yes, mother and I had attic rooms. Mistress Gordon's rooms were in the east wing, Master Gordon's, the west wing. The two women didn't see each other. We knew our place and never entered the white woman's world. She had her own house slaves. You're shocked, but that is the way in the Islands."

Feeling caught, Sarah looked toward the open door.

Kechi walked to the window and watched the children playing happily together. Hugging herself she returned to the table. "My mother taught me the Igbo ways. We believe God in charge. My name, whatever God gives, reminds me to accept everything God puts in my life. After we die, we'll be born again, babes back into our families. I miss my mother as she misses her family, their plantation, the many rivers, and the thick forest's fertile soil. But when this life ends, we'll return to her family in Nigeria. Knowing this gives me hope."

Literally born, again? Sarah's church didn't teach that concept. It sounded outlandish, but Kechi gave her no time to ponder.

"I married Coby, his name a kinda tree. Mother said same kinda tree in Nigeria and Jamaica. Its wood dark brown that how my man got his name. He one a my father's field slaves. He know how ta nurture the ground and grow sweet potatoes in Jamaica.

We teach our girls to grow sweet potatoes and I tell 'em stories about my mother's home and family. I want 'em to know Igbo ways. Want 'em to know their ancestors love 'em no matter where they are or what they doin'."

Kechi stared wistfully for just a moment and then continued, "Five years ago my father became ill and died. His will freed my mother, husband, daughters, and me. My father wanted all of us to come to New Jersey, but my mother refused to leave. She said she had never left his home and she wouldn't leave his grave. Father had bought this land from his cousin Thomas Gordon who welcomed us with open arms."

"You're Thomas Gordon's cousin?"

"That right. Do you know him?"

"I know who he is, James and I work for a friend of his, Mr. Mudie."

"Yes, I've met him." Kechi continued with her story, "Coby figure how to coax sweet potatoes out of this cold ground, we sell 'em. But as you saw, people ain't eager to try 'em."

Sarah couldn't help but laugh, "Yes, I know the feeling, but I'm so glad I took the chance. We love the new flavor and besides now I have you for a friend."

Joining in the laughter, Kechi agreed, "Yes, I'm happy we're friends. And the children get along."

Sarah placed her empty teacup and spoon in the wash tub as she said, "They'll want to come back again I'm sure."

"Good, why don't you bring James and come for Sunday evenin' meal?" Cup in hand, Kechi led Sarah out the door.

"That would be wonderful," Sarah waved the children to her as she walked toward Lulu chomping grass near Kechi's cabin.

Later pondering Kechi's story Sarah tried to put it into a frame of time that she could understand. From what she could determine Kechi could be a few years younger than she. That meant Kechi's mother had been maybe sixteen when snatched from her family. How awful that would be for a young, innocent girl. Sarah marveled at how well Kechi's mother had lived her life. Through all her struggles, she kept the faith and beliefs her family had taught her and passed them on to her daughter.

Kechi and Sarah became good friends and found time away from the market to visit. They shared feelings, hopes, and beliefs with one another, as Sarah learned to serve sweet potatoes boiled, mashed, fried, in pies, biscuits, stews, soups, and even in her cake recipe for special occasions.

October 1694

Thomas Gordon had been appointed Deputy Secretary and Register of the East New Jersey Proprietors Group two years earlier, and as his life moved forward with more professional success he was often approached by available women. Some of the women were subtle and some direct. However, he remained single and absorbed in his work.

He attended the Annual Governor's Harvest Ball each October where he was invariably surrounded by single women, widows, and mothers of available daughters. He was kind, but never led any of the women on to think he was interested in romance. He socialized with everyone in attendance and danced with many women. In sixteen-ninety-four he was in attendance at the ball before the Mudie family arrived.

When the family was announced everyone's head turned, anxious to see the gowns the young women wore. Thomas also watched. He was astounded when he realized the most beautiful among them was not an unknown visitor but was Janet. He could hardly believe his eyes. The child was gone. He was staring at a desirable woman.

Gordon greeted the family and as they dispersed through the crowd. His height allowed a view over the heads of the crowd. He watched Janet. She had kept her petite frame but grown into womanhood. She moved with self-assurance. He watched as she conversed comfortably with both women and men. She gave each person her undivided attention and easily drew out their interest and delight. Once Gordon was able to make his way to Janet's side, he asked her to dance. She lifted herself onto her tiptoes, smiled into his face, and accepted his invitation.

Early that December, the ground covered in snow, Sarah kept fires alight in every room of the Mudie home. While the sisters were out making social calls, Sarah worked in Janet's dressing area brushing her frocks and mending stockings. Thinking she'd be alone for at least an hour she was startled when she heard the room's door handle rattle. She turned to see Janet collapse onto the bed.

"Janet, why aren't you with your sisters? Are you ill? Shall I fetch the doctor?"

"No, Sarah, I'm not ill. I couldn't bear another moment with the boring small talk and excused myself with a headache."

Confused Sarah asked, "But you don't have a headache?"

"No, I do not have a headache." She signed and almost swooning, sang, "I'm in love."

Sarah smiled remembering the wonderful feelings associated with first love. "And who is the lucky young man?"

Janet sat up with excitement in her eye, "Oh, my love is not a young man."

"What?" Sarah sat on the bed next to Janet. "You're in love with some old codger? Have you lost your mind? Janet, you're only twenty-one you don't want to spend your youth playing nursemaid to an elderly husband. What will your father say?"

"Sarah, he's not that old, he's only forty-two and quite healthy." Her eyes twinkled with delight. Hugging herself Janet went on, "Oh, Sarah, isn't love wonderful? Is this the way you feel about James? Do you get that funny feeling in your innards when he looks at you?"

Sarah laughed. "Well, yes, that does sound like love. At least what I know of it." Sarah stood to return to her duties. "I have found that over the years it has simmered down some, but my desires have become stronger and my love for James deeper. I'm sure it will be the same for you."

"I hope not. I want to feel like this forever." Janet put her feet on the floor and danced around the room.

Sarah smiled. "So, does your family know and approve? The difference in your ages is the number of years you've been on this earth. That sounds like a big gap to me. You need to take some time before you make such a decision. Your actions could make you miserable the rest of your life."

"Or make my life pleasurable and full of joy. As far as my family is concerned, if they don't know, it is because they are blind, but my love will speak with my father very soon. We plan a Christmas wedding." She signed. "And, Sarah, I need your help preparing. It has to be the most special day of my life."

Laughing, Sarah reassured her, "I'm sure it will be, Janet." Then becoming serious Sarah asked, "Are you going to tell me who has your heart so tightly gripped?"

"Of course. Who else would it be, but Thomas?"

"Thomas? Which Thomas? There are several in your social circle."

Janet twirled around the room, "Thomas Gordon, of course, we have been in love since he took me in his arms at the Governor's Harvest Ball. He has pledged his eternal love to me. And I do love him so."

And their wedding, amongst the decorations of Christmas ribbons and candles, was like the happy ending to a fairy tale.

···

Eger to share his good news, Thomas Gordon wrote to his brother.

January 1695

Dearest John,

I hope this epistle finds your family in good health.
I am writing with good news, in fact, the best news
I've been able to share in these past eight years.

Once again, I enjoy the bliss of marriage with a
wonderful woman. You might remember Mudie's
young daughter, Janet. I know you are seeing her in
your mind's eye as a child, but let me assure you,
she is a lovely, mature woman who has captured
my heart.

My happiness has given me a new determination to
make East New Jersey a place where its citizens
can live in peace and safety.

I close with my heart full. — Thomas

March 1695

One day while Sarah and the boys visited Kechi, she gave Sarah seedlings and explained how to plant them in a hill of soil with space between the seedlings the length of Kechi's foot. "First heart-shaped leaves will grow on the vine. Then come beautiful, purple, and white morning glory flowers. The root grow to delicious sweet potatoes. In Jamaica they done in four moons, but here frost comes, kills plants. Cover 'em at night during the third moon." Patting Sarah on the back, Kechi promised, "Soon you be Nnenne with your own plantation."

Sarah laughed, but felt proud to be accepted into Kechi's family of women plantation managers.

As Kechi explained to Sarah how to cure the potatoes so they'd store through the winter, Sarah read distress in Kechi's eyes. In a firm tone Sarah ordered Kechi, "Sit down. I'll make some tea." As she poured the steaming water into the cups, Sarah watched Kechi wring her apron in her hands, "What has you upset? Tell me, maybe I can help."

Kechi slumped into a chair and whispered, "Folk say slave catchers headin' this way."

"Slave catchers?" Sarah placed a cup in front of Kechi. "But you're free you don't need to worry."

"Yes, we free. We have papers, but catchers don't stop to read 'em. They grab any black man, woman, or child. Take 'em to a slave owner. Collect reward. Coby tell me not to fret, but I do. I do." Tears streamed down her smooth brown face "And there nothin' you or anyone can do to stop 'em."

Sarah ignored her tea and hugged Kechi to her bosom.

∎∎∎

When James entered their cabin that evening, he found Sarah pacing its length, deep crevices in her brow, tears glistening in her eyes. "Sarah, what's happened? Are the boys all right?"

"Oh, James, you startled me. Yes, the boys are fine. It's Kechi, she's heard that slave catchers are coming to Perth Amboy. She's frantic at the thought of her girls being taken from her. James, we must do something. We have to save her children."

James wrapped his arms around his wife and held her tight against his chest. "Sarah, Sarah." he whispered in her ear as he rocked her like an upset infant. She rested her head on his shoulder and surrendered to his strength. Once she calmed, James spoke softly, "Sarah, you know there's nothing we can do. There's no law to protect free Negros. Blacks are seen as property. Slave hunters don't care if the Negroes they catch are runaways or free and authorities don't get in their way. All you can do is pray for their protection."

Sarah wept silent tears against James' rough shirt, "I know, but I feel so helpless. It's not fair. Laws should protect all free citizens no matter their color. What would we do if the law took our children away from us? I think I'd die."

Slave Catchers

As always Perth Amboy market day vendors parked their selling carts in a haphazard way not in neat rows as Sarah remembered them in Haarlem. Kechi always set up in the corner as far from the Slave Block as she could. But today the corner sat empty. Sarah wandered from cart to cart through the web of paths, confused in the labyrinth. *Where can Kechi be?*

A sharp, November wind from the sea caught Sarah's bonnet. She looked skyward as she held it to her head. Dark, grey clouds gathered offshore. This time of year, a storm from the ocean could mean a nor'easter. The least of that would be strong winds and heavy rain, the worst, trees down, buildings damaged, people hurt. She needed to get to shelter before it made landfall.

Sarah quickened her step back to Kechi's usual spot, the area still empty. Sarah approached the man selling beans nearby. "Excuse me, sir, have you seen the black woman who usually sells sweet potatoes over there?" she pointed to the empty space.

"Not taday. No sign ah 'er. You'll not get strange taters taday, Missus." Shoving a bag of beans toward Sarah, he continued, "How 'bout beans? These ar' best 'round."

She stammered, "No . . . no, thank you," as she turned and hurried away.

Kechi wouldn't miss a market day. Something must be wrong. *What should I do?* Sarah thought about going home trusting no harm had befallen her friend. However, she couldn't shake the feeling that Kechi might be in danger. But how could she help? Hands shaking, knees weak, she had to do something. *But what?* She straightened her back and walked with purpose along Water Street away from the market.

Forehead furrowed, head down, and shoulders crunched forward, Sarah ran square into Margaret and Issy Mudie. Brought back to the present, Sarah stuttered, "Oh . . . I . . . I'm . . . so sorry. So sorry," as she ran away from the girls.

■■■

"Something's amiss. Sarah's never rude," commented Margaret as she regained her balance.

"Maybe we can help." Issy offered as she made sure her hat was as it should be.

"Not now, we have shopping to do for tonight's special guests" Margaret giggled, "Remember Horace is to announce our engagement" and they hurried on with their errands.

Issy tried to keep up, "You're right. Besides, we need to finish before the storm arrives."

"I shouldn't have been so impertinent to the Mudie sisters." Sarah muttered to herself. Almost running, Sarah turned up Market Street toward Kechi's, hoping to get there before the storm. Sarah chided herself, I'm on a fool's errand. I'll find her at home safe with her family. Out of breath and with a stitch in her side she heard a commotion, sounding like a battle, before she saw the struggle.

Children crying out for their mother. A woman's shrill voice keening in agony. A man's bass voice shouting orders. Sarah rushed toward the scene. Breathless, she froze in place, watching. A muscular white man unknown to Sarah tore Kechi's daughters from her arms and threw them into the back of a horse drawn cart. Shouting orders to his cronies standing nearby, he yelled, "Hold them two pickaninnies. Don't let 'em get away. Go, now. I'll catch up after I take care of this Niggress banshee."

Sarah couldn't believe her eyes or ears. The horse galloped away with the cart carrying the wailing Acuchi and Udo. The man held Kechi so she couldn't follow, but Kechi didn't give up. Struggling against his strength she freed an arm and reached for his face. She scratched deep bloody stripes down his jowls. He tried to move his face out of her reach but couldn't in time. Kechi grabbed at him again. This time her fingernails found an eye.

The man screamed in pain, pushed Kechi away, and then rounded a fist into her jaw. She landed in a heap. Continuing his savage attack, he kicked her in the stomach and head. A streak of lightening lit the sky. Deafening thunder rocked the ground.

"Kechi! Kechi!" Sarah screamed as she ran to her friend who lay in a pool of blood. Sarah didn't see the savage man raise his arm. He swung and backhanded her on the side of her head. She fell to her knees. She couldn't see or hear anything. *Am I dying?*

Before Sarah found her answer, he lifted her by one arm and pushed her toward his last remaining underling, "Don't need no white woman interferin'. Take 'er back to town." Then he walked to his horse, mounted, and rode south.

Sarah kicked and flailed her arms, but the man held her tight. She couldn't break free. Another blow, this time to the back of her head. No pain, only darkness.

...

Coming to, Sarah found herself lying in a narrow passageway. Her clothing rain soaked, hair stringing into her face. Thick fog and mist obscured her view. Sitting up, she held her head in her hands. She'd never had such pain or experienced such intense fear. She couldn't fathom anyone being as cruel as those men had been. Befuddled, she didn't recognize her surroundings.

As her mind cleared, she heard men's loud cursing and women giggling. The stench of wet dirt mingled with animal and human waste turned her stomach. She needed to get away from this vile place, but before she could rise a heavy-set drunken sailor swayed toward her.

"Whasa pretty lady doin' out in 'is weather?" He staggered, then fell against the side of the building. "Come in and have a drink wit' me."

129

Sarah realized she had been dumped behind a tavern near the docks. *I must get home.* She sat up, bent her knees, and dug her heels into the mud. With her hands behind her, palms flat on the ground, she tried scooting away from the drunk, but her body would not move fast enough. He lurched forward and spewed vomit on the hem of her dress and shoes.

No time to test her strength, Sarah stood to run, but her shoes slipped and slid on the muddy ground. Thankfully, the ruffian, too inebriated to follow, staggered away. Dizzy and weak, she made her way toward James and safety.

...

James, beside himself with worry, had fed the boys supper and put them to bed. He couldn't imagine where Sarah might be at this late hour. He didn't know what to do or how to find her. He paced the road in front of their cabin looking each way, searching through the darkness for his wife.

Thick fog obscured his view. He'd forgotten both coat and hat. His clothing damp he shivered against the cold but wouldn't leave his vigil. At long last he saw a bent figure struggling toward him. He heard a whimper. *Is that Sarah? Has she been hurt? Yes.* He saw his wife staggering forward hugging herself. *She must be freezing.*

He rushed through the fog to her side. Sarah folded into his arms, "Sarah, what happened?"

"Slave Catchers . . ."

"What did they do to you? Did they—"

"No. No. James, nothing like that," she let him carry her into their cabin.

Although feeling inadequate for the task, he tended to her needs. Sarah had always been the nurturer. He didn't know where to begin healing her physical or emotional wounds. Jaw ridged, he held back an intense desire to avenge her injuries.

Sarah wept as James helped her undress and wash vomit, mud, and dried blood from her face, hands, and legs. He didn't push for answers to the agonizing questions swirling in his mind. She'd explain in her own time.

Once in her nightgown, sipping from a cup of hot, strong, sweet-tea she explained what had happened. James stifled his first reaction. Reprimanding her for her rash actions wouldn't change the outcome. His arm around her shoulders he comforted her as best he could while he listened to her tearful tale.

"The slave catchers took Kechi's girls. Then their leader beat Kechi for trying to protect them." Sarah, shuddered, "I'm sure she's dead. I tremble to think what might happen to the girls. How can people be so cruel? James, why does God allow such evil?"

"You need to sleep." James held her elbow and walked her to their bed. He pulled down the quilt and waited for her to lie down. Tucking the quilt around her chin he whispered, "Sarah, I'm sorry, I have no answers." He blew out the candle, settled himself beside her, and fell asleep.

■■■

Lying in the dark listening to James' quiet snores, Sarah ached for her friend. She couldn't imagine the pain a mother would feel having her children taken from her. Kechi didn't measure time as the colonist did, but Sarah judged the girls to be between ten and eight years of age. *They're so innocent and beautiful. What kind of life will they have?*

Sarah couldn't bear her anguish. She clutched the edge of the quilt in her fist. Fierce hatred of those slave catchers gripped her heart. Christ said, 'Pray for your enemies.' Maybe someday, she thought, but no, not tonight. Tonight, she would ask God to bring down His wrath upon them.

Her only solace was remembering Kechi's belief that she'd be reborn an infant back with her Nigerian family. She'd be home and safe waiting for her girls. Sarah rolled closer to James using his body heat for comfort. Looking out the window she whispered to the night sky, "Oh, God, wherever Kechi and her children are, please comfort them."

···

James woke before dawn and eased away from Sarah's warmth into the cold bedroom air. He dressed without a sound to not disturb Sarah and tiptoed to the wood pile. He carried logs to the hearth and after stacking them over kindling, lit a fire and waited until it took. Then grabbing his jacket and hat he left the cabin walking in fast, long strides toward Kechi's.

Turning the corner from Water Street unto Westminster James saw Kechi pounding on Thomas Gordon's front door. He heard her sobs, pleading for help, "Thomas, please." As

James entered the scene the door opened, and Gordon welcomed them in. James put his arm around Kechi's shoulders until she stopped shivering and quaking. She looked rough with bruises on her face and dried blood in her hair. He noticed she stooped forward. He supposed she had pain from being kicked.

As soon as Kechi could speak, she told her cousin, "Slave Catchers take my girls. Coby rode off with his rifle as soon as he learned what happened. I might lose them all. Please help me."

James found even the thought of having children snatched too painful to think of what anyone could do to help. But Gordon didn't hesitate. "Kechi, did they say where they were taking them?"

Kechi's words stabbed the air, "The catchers said they were going back to the Carolinas. How will we ever get the girls back?"

Gordon spoke with compassion, but also authority, "Kechi, you were right to come to me. I'll send riders out. I have contacts in the Carolinas. I'll put the word out."

"Bless you, Thomas, bless you."

"Now you go home in case Coby returns with the girls." Gordon ran his hand through his hair, "I'll dress and be on my way. If my men see Coby, they'll send him home. The Carolinas are not safe for him and he should be with you." Leading them to the door he continued, "Now, go home. I'll send my cook Lucy over to help you." Gordon put his hand on

James' back and asked, "James, can you stay with her until Lucy gets there?"

"Yes sir, I will. Thank you for your help."

Kechi let James escort her back to her cabin. He lit a fire in her hearth, filled the kettle with water and hung it over the flames. Kechi placed cups on the table and put tea leaves into the ceramic tea pot, a routine she didn't have to think about. Then she sat, elbows on the table, holding her head in her hands. She did not cry. She stared at the homespun tablecloth with vacant eyes.

James brought in firewood and filled the water bucket, then poured the boiling water from the kettle over the tea leaves. He poured the steeped tea through a strainer then spooned sugar into one of the cups. Stirring the sugared tea, he set it on the table in front of Kechi.

As she sipped the tea, James commented, "Lucy will cook breakfast when she gets here. You need to eat. You don't want to get yourself sick. Your family needs you to be strong for them."

"I know, James, I know." She seemed calmed by the tea's warmth and sweetness.

They sat in silence. Nothing could be said to ease Kechi's pain. Two quick knocks on the door startled them both. Before either could react, Lucy stepped into the cabin carrying a basket. The sweet aroma of fresh baked bread wafted all around her. James thanked her for coming and excused himself.

...

When James returned home, he found Sarah at the hearth preparing porridge. "Where have you been? I've been worried sick."

"I woke early and went to offer my help to Kechi and Coby. On the way I saw Kechi pounding on Gordon's door. Seems Coby took off after the slave catchers. Kechi heard them mention the Carolinas. Gordon's going to send riders to find Coby and send him home, then to track down the kidnappers."

"Good. Do you think Gordon's men will find the girls and get them back?"

"Don't know, but let's hope they can. Gordon said he has contacts along the coast. He'll send word to them. Hopefully, they'll help locate the girls."

"I'll pray for their safe return. How is Kechi?"

"She's upset, of course. I walked her home and stayed with her until Gordon's cook, Lucy, arrived. She brought fresh baked bread and eggs to cook. Kechi will be well taken care of."

"Thank goodness."

...

Two days later Coby returned, two weeks later Gordon's men came back empty handed. They couldn't find the girls or any leads on where they might have been taken. Persistent, Gordon didn't give up. He wrote to his contacts every week. He knew firsthand the pain of losing beloved children.

Kechi and Coby carried on the best they could. In time they gave into their heartache and stopped searching the horizon for their lost daughters.

The Voorlezer's House

In January Sarah baked one of those special sweet potato confections for the party at Gordons' to wish fair sailing to Janet, Thomas, and their eleven-month-old son Andrew. Gordon had been called to England to meet with the proprietors over the lack of rents being collected. Although he hoped to mediate an agreement that would give aid to the tenants and still reap profits for the proprietors.

Then in April a sad event left James grieving. "Sarah, I feel like I've lost my father all over again. David Mudie treated me with respect, gave me advice, and brought me to America . . . to you and the life we have together. I'll miss him."

She placed her hand on his, "I know. The boys thought of him as a grandfather. We all feel his absence."

April 1696

Dearest Janet,

I am so deeply sorry for your loss. Your father was a good man. His death has left an emptiness in our lives. He was like a father to James and a grandpa to the boys. I'll look in on your sisters often, so don't worry about them. Take care of yourself and Andrew. Give Thomas our best.

I continue to remember you and yours in my prayers.
Your Friend — Sarah

...

A few weeks later, Sarah prepared James' favorite meal, fed the boys, and put them to bed early. She needed James' undivided attention while he enjoyed her venison stew cooked with turnips, rutabagas, and sweet potatoes in a thick, creamy gravy. "James, today I heard about a group of Dutch families settling on Staten Island. They need a Master Blacksmith. It'll be close to New York City and set on two rivers for travel and shipping goods. They say it's in a safe area and will grow fast."

James' undivided attention focused on his plate, not Sarah, "This stew is better than your best. I'm almost too full to enjoy a piece of that apple pie I smell."

Exasperated, Sarah sighed, "Oh, James, aren't you paying any attention to what I'm saying?"

James stopped eating. Fork midair, he stared at Sarah sitting next to him at the table, "I heard you talk about a Dutch settlement on Staten Island. So . . ."

Sarah jumped into his hesitation, "I think you should talk to the founders. I think a new place would help you enjoy life again. When we met you seemed happy to be one of the founding workers here in Perth Amboy. I liked your enthusiasm for the community. Since Mudie's passing you've lost that."

Looking down at the gravy left on his plate, he answered flatly, "I don't know. We're doing all right here and I don't speak Dutch. It'd be like going to a foreign country."

"Don't worry about the language. I can help you. You'll catch on in no time." She placed her hand on his arm, "I want my entertaining James back. The fun man I fell in love with. I want joy back in our home."

James rose from the table and turned to Sarah. Putting his arm around her shoulders he said, "Don't get up, I'll get the pie."

She shook her head showing him her exasperation, "Thank you, but what say you about the new settlement?"

Returning to her side with the pie in hand, he bent and kissed her cheek, "I'll look into it if that's what you want." He winked at her, "You know I like to make you happy." James sat back down at the table and once again focused on his plate.

James wanted to be loyal to the man who brought him to his happy life in America. He'd planned to stay on as Master Blacksmith in Perth Amboy and raise his family. But Sarah was right. Since Mudie died, James hadn't been himself and he didn't know how to remedy his discomfort. When Sarah suggested they might leave, James welcomed the relief that swept over him.

■■■

After sharing their plans with family and friends, James and Sarah happily packed their sparse belongings and by mid-June they were on their way. Frank, Sarah's youngest sister Emily's husband, helped them haul the load to the Staten Island Ferry dock. The boys hung onto the rail of the ferry searching the depth of the Arthur Kil Sound naming each variety of fish. "Look, Papa, there's a Striped Bass." "I see a Bluefish and a Porgy." Even five-year-old Sany chimed in, "Look, Mama, a long eel."

After disembarking, James hired a man with an ox and rough, wooden two-wheeled cart for the last leg of their journey. While the boys took turns riding on top of the load, James and Sarah walked behind keeping an eye on them. A cloudy day offered relief from the high summer sun.

Cockles Town, a small settlement compared to the city of Perth Amboy, sat along Arthur Kil which ran downstream to the Raritan River, flowed past Perth Amboy, and into the Atlantic Ocean. On a low hill along the river James built a forge with living quarters above, not large but adequate for the family of five. He constructed the building from local oak timber, then faced the forge with river-rocks the family had gathered.

Fitchett's House and Forge, Cockles Town

Self-employed, James answered to no one but himself. He liked that. As soon as the forge proved successful, James took on an apprentice to teach as Mr. Ramsey had taught him. Louis Du Bois' father paid James for the young man's room, board, and training. The added income helped replace what Sarah had contributed to the rent as the Mudie's assistant housekeeper.

The Fitchett boys had plenty of land to roam looking for adventure. They'd heard about Captain Kidd's pirate exploits and spent hours using hickory sticks as swords to subdue imaginary invaders. Hearing stories about Kidd burying his booty on Staten Island, they dug holes in the surrounding forest determined to find a chest filled with jewels and gold.

James found the spyglass his father had given him and told his family about the day he'd received it. "It was my third birthday when my father gave me this spyglass and showed me how to use it. He took it to my bedroom window and explained, 'Here, James, put the small end in front of one eye and your hand over the other eye. Now, point the bigger end at the window.'

"When I followed his instructions, he encouraged me on, 'Yes. Good. What do you see?'

"I told him, 'I see trees, birds, houses. And there's Mama's rose garden'"

"He laughed. I was pointing the big end down. He urged me on, 'Good. Good. Now point it up and over there.'

"I had to move the spyglass away from my eye to see what direction father was pointing. But then putting the spyglass back in place, I positioned it higher and to the right, 'Father, I see your fishing boat. It's at the dock.'"

The boys laughed as they pictured their father trying to maneuver the spyglass correctly.

James went on, "I learned to recognize the large dark-blue M-O-R-A-N painted on the side of my father's fishing boat, before I learned my ABCs.

"Every day after my lessons, I'd station myself at my bedroom window like a sentry. On clear days I could see the busy Montrose harbor and I watched ships sail in and out from the Baltic Sea, France, Portugal and even from here, the American Colonies."

His sons lost interest in his tale, but he smiled as he remembered how as soon as he saw the Moran, he'd run through the house shouting, Father's home, Father's home. He wouldn't stop until he stood on the dock to greet him and celebrate his homecoming. As an adult he realized that everyone in Montrose must have known when the Moran returned to port whenever they saw him running toward the docks with his mother trying to keep up. Life had always been happier with his father's return.

Once he was old enough to go to the harbor alone, he'd carry his spyglass to the bank of South Esk Channel and spy on sailors as their ships arrived. He often wondered how it would feel to sail out of the Montrose harbor to a far-offshore, but he knew his Mother would never allow that. He no longer needed to wonder, his voyage had brought him Sarah and the family he loved with all his heart.

Young James took to the spyglass right away and searched the horizon for pirates every day.

Sarah settled more comfortably in the Dutch community than she had with the Scots in Perth Amboy. She spoke Dutch to their children and kept traditions passed down through generations of her family. James shared a few Scottish customs with the family. And, as citizens of America, they added a variety of countries' customs they had learned from their Perth Amboy neighbors including some from the Lenape Indians who had welcomed the new arrivals to their land.

Cockles Town grew to about one-hundred-twenty cabins with a population of almost seven-hundred-fifty. The men met each month in an Elder's barn to discuss expansion plans. Strong cider served, the men spoke in loud and sometimes slurred voices. Every so often an animal answered with a neigh or bleat. James could follow most discussions, but over critical matters he relied on Dirk, a townsman who could translate for him. During one meeting the men talked of adding a Voorlezer's house. James spoke up, "I'm sorry, I'm a bit confused, Dirk, please explain what they're talking about."

"Of course. In Dutch communities the Voorlezer is an educated man who teaches children during the week and leads the Sunday community worship. The proposal is to buy a house and hire a Voorlezer. Every family will sign the deed promising to pay a share of the expenses."

"Oh, all right. Thanks. They're not going to build a house?"

"No, there's a suitable house nearby that we can buy and move closer to the center of town. That way it will be put to use sooner than building another from the ground up."

"That makes sense. Will the Voorlezer teach in English?"

Before Dirk could answer, the Elders, who understood James' question, murmured to one another. Those in charge ended the meeting saying a final decision would be made next month.

...

As usual, Sarah waited up for James' return to learn what the men had discussed and decided. She greeted James at the cabin door with open arms and a kiss.

James saw the eager look on her face, eyes wide and brow raised, but he couldn't match her enthusiasm. With drooping shoulders, he walked to his chair near the hearth and let his body drop onto it.

Following behind she asked, "James, what is it? Is there trouble or sickness?"

Staring into the flames James assured her. "No. Nothing like that."

Sarah put her hand on his shoulder and lowered herself onto a low three-legged wooden stool beside James' feet.

Holding his face between her hands she turned his head to face her. "Then what is it? You look discouraged."

Taking her hands in his and pulling them to his lap, James explained about the Voorlezer's House.

"I know." Sarah said. "The women have been urging their husbands. This settlement must have a school and place of worship."

"Yes, I agree."

Searching his face for answers she asked, "Then what's your concern?"

"The Voorlezer will teach in Dutch."

"Of course."

James let go of Sarah's hands, stood, and began pacing the oval rag-rug Sarah had braided. "Sarah, this land is no longer the New Netherlands. It's New York. We're citizens of an English colony. All the children, not just ours, need to learn English."

Sarah stood and met James as he rounded back toward her, "You want that because English is your language."

Holding both Sarah's shoulders in his hands he exclaimed, "No, Sarah, Scots fought hard to push England out of our country, but in the end, we lost and England rules. This new land will be the same. The Dutch could not overcome the English either.

"Sarah, eight years ago William, your Dutch King and his English wife, Mary, became the rulers of both The Netherlands and England. This land will always be ruled by

English monarchs. Learning English and Dutch will benefit the children. Let families speak Dutch at home and in community gatherings if they like. But if the Dutch don't learn the King's English they'll not succeed, and Cockles Town will die."

"Did you say this tonight at the meeting?"

"I only questioned what language the Voorlezer will teach. Glares and disagreeable murmurings filled the room. Then the meeting ended, and I left."

Sarah stepped back, away from James's grip, "James, this is a Dutch settlement. You knew that before we came, and you didn't say anything about the children being taught in English."

"I thought you'd continue teaching the boys at home." James' brow creased with confusion. "I'd never heard of a Voorlezer before tonight."

...

The following month the men again discussed their plan. The Dutchmen expressed their wish to remain isolated, their language and customs intact. James understood, but could remain silent no longer. When they allowed him to speak, he said, "I understand your desires, but we live in an English colony now. My children speak Dutch and English. We keep Dutch customs, but this community needs to look to the future. If our children are to succeed in this new land, they must know the language of the government. I can't in clear conscious sign the deed unless the children are taught in English."

Dirk made sure everyone present understood James' words. However, no one supported his concerns.

A sudden wind whirled straw around the barn floor. The leader of the group answered, "James, we need you to support a Voorlezer and the house. Stop being so stubborn. We are a Dutch community. We speak Dutch and so do our children. We have no need to learn English."

The night sky lit up and the sound of thunder rattled in the distance. "That's fine. This is a Dutch community and we all live together and do business in the Dutch language. But just outside Cockles Town's boundaries is a very English land. The ruling government is English. Business must be conducted in English out there.

"Do you honestly believe your children will remain here speaking only Dutch forever? Do you think only the Dutch will ever come into your settlement? Keeping your language and customs is admirable and right within your homes, but if you don't teach your children English, they'll be shunned and limited in their ability to support themselves and their families.

"Early settlers welcomed people from all corners of the world. Everyone can keep their language and customs to themselves or share them with their neighbors, but the English are not going away. They will be here forever. You must see that speaking English in public matters is the only way any of us will survive. I'm a Scot, I would rather be free of English rule, but that's not possible. We must all accept that reality."

A sudden crack of thunder startled the men as torrential rain burst from the sky.

■■■

Everyday a different man stopped by the forge attempting to sway James' thinking to agree with the majority. Raised voices could be heard whenever the talk became heated. Women avoided Sarah and didn't allow their children to play with the Fitchett boys. Sarah lamented, "An adult argument carried on through the children isn't fair. It isn't right."

"I know, I never expected so much hostility. I feel sick but can't go along with their plan. I'm sorry."

Once Sarah understood James' concerns, she agreed with him. She liked the way he kept to his ideals. Sarah spent evenings comforting him, "James you have nothing to be sorry for. You're right and I admire you for standing your ground." As they hugged one another she whispered, "We'll see this through together."

■■■

In time the settlement leaders admitted that realized they couldn't support the Voorlezer's house without James' financial help. The harvest completed and winter on its way, even as the reluctant Elders gave in and agreed to his stipulation, James hoped they would soon understand his reasoning.

Next to his signature James wrote "children will be taught in Dutch and English." With this act James agreed to add money to the project, completing the transaction.

At home James took Sarah in his arms. "Ramsay told me once that I could change the world around me. I didn't believe him then. But now I see that I have."

"Yes, James, you have made this New World a better place for the future of many children." She lifted her head into his kiss. "I'm proud of you."

James and his neighbor James Hanse Dye each donated a portion of their land that sat at the corner of Arthur Kil Road and Center Street. Men appointed by the Elders moved the house to that site which was just south of Fitchett's forge. They placed the two-story wood frame building on two-foot thick foundation walls made of fieldstones with mud mortar making a cellar. The entrance door on the south end led to the room where the Voorlezer prepared meals.

Voorlezer's House, Cockles Town

The first and second floors each had a fireplace and one small room in the north-west corner. The Voorlezer used that space on the first floor as a sitting room and the second floor for sleeping. The Community used the large area on the main level for worship services and located the school room upstairs. Wide white-pine boards finished the floors on both stories. Cockles Town had a school, church, and Voorlezer.

Basic rules for the Voorlezer included:

School shall begin in the morning at 8 o'clock and end at 11 o'clock then begin again in the afternoon from one to four o'clock.

At the opening of School the Voorlezer shall have one of the children read the morning prayer as it stands in the catechism. School shall close with the prayer before meals. In the afternoon it shall open with the prayer after meals and close with the evening prayer.

The Voorlezer shall also keep the church clean and ring the bell three times before the meeting. Before the sermon he shall read a chapter of the Holy Scriptures then the Ten Commandments and the Creed and then lead in singing.

The Voorlezer shall provide a basin of water for the Holy Baptism. He shall provide bread and wine for the Holy supper at the church's expense.

The Voorlezer shall be discreet, temperate and industrious and patient with the children and affable in their instruction.

He shall invite the people to funerals and dig the graves and toll the bell. He can visit other towns that do not have a Voorlezer.

*The Voorlezer receives a yearly salary, free house
rent and use of the garden and house lot belonging to
the school.*

Because James Fitchett wrote a note on the deed at his
signature, Cockles Town added another rule:

The Voorlezer will teach in Dutch and English.

That December Sarah wrote to Janet:

*I didn't have time to write before we moved. We are
now living in Cockles Town on Staten Island. The
town got its name because there are oysters and
clams aplenty in fresh kil waters. James is doing well
as master blacksmith and has an apprentice to help.*

*This is a Dutch community. James convinced the
town's Elders to have the Voorlezer teach the
children in both Dutch and English. It was a struggle,
but he feels all the children need English to live in the
colonies. As a bonus James and our neighbor Mr.
Dye have contracted to supply the Voorlezer with
firewood for the next fifty-years. To keep that promise
I'm sure the boys will need to take over felling timber
once James is too old.*

*Before we left Perth Amboy, I asked your neighbor
Mrs. Duncan to look in on your sisters often until you
return.*

*I hope Thomas is successful with his business
dealings there in England. I've heard there is some
trouble brewing back in New Jersey.*

*Do you know how long Thomas will be required to be
in England? I'm sure you want to return to your
sisters.*

*The boys miss you and Andrew. They ask when they
can see you again. I can't seem to explain the sense
of time to their young minds.*

I miss you and our talks. My prayers are with you.

Sarah

The Fitchetts settled into a family routine in Cockles Town.
Business from the forge allowed them the necessary comforts.
They had friends. Sarah and the children attended Sunday
services in the Voorlezer's house where the older boys also
attended school during the week. James played tunes on his tin
whistle and taught his children bouncy songs and ballads of
love and loss. Sarah, of course, taught them songs to worship
God.

The home rang with:

> *"The Parting Glass"*
> *But since it fell into my lot*
> *That I should rise and you should not*
> *I'll gently rise and softly call*
> *"Good night and joy be to you all*

> *"Ward the Pirate"*
> *Come all you gallant seamen bold,*
> *All you that march to drum,*
> *Let's go and look for Captain Ward,*
> *Far on the sea he roams.*
> *He is the biggest robber*
> *That ever you did hear,*
> *there's not been such a robber found*

For above this hundred year.

And words of the psalms:

Some trust in chariots, and some in horses,
but we will remember the name of the Lord our God.

Create in me, O God, a pure heart
And give me a new and right spirit.
Do not drive me away from your presence
And do not remove your holy spirit from me.
Comfort me once more with your help
And with your joyful spirit sustain me.

James watched Sarah in the dim candlelight mending children's clothing worn thin. He remembered watching his mother stitch decorative items to enhance their lovely home. That house had been originally built by his grandparents and his mother inherited it. It was a wonderful place to grow up—secure and cozy. Tomes with wonders of the world, maps, and adventure stories filled bookcases, just the things to alight a young boy's imagination. The family had servants to prepare meals, clean the house, and maintain the grounds. However, James' mother insisted on tending her little summer rose garden, her pride and joy.

Sarah worked hard and made do with what little they had. There was never enough money to get ahead or buy extras, no fancy stitching to beautify her home. Sarah kept their children busy working in the garden and the cabin, teaching them the satisfaction of an honest day's work. In the evenings, while she mended and sewed, Sarah listened to the children read from the Bible and presided over their writing and cipher practice. Sarah never complained, but James wanted more for her. He longed to give her a life like his mother's.

Meanwhile, Sarah and Janet exchanged letters as often as possible as they each carried out their demanding responsibilities.

March 1696
London, England

Dear Sarah,

I'm looking forward to experiencing the London I've heard so much about. Thomas has promised it all to me. I love him so. The one thing I have heard is that London's summers are unbearable.

Thank goodness, Mr. Dockwra, a former proprietor, will set up a meeting in Yorkshire, July next year. There will be clean country air and cooler temperatures, and best of all Scots will have less distance to travel. Thomas said he thinks most of the Group will attend. He's keen to see his brother, John. We'll enjoy his company outside of the meetings.

Thomas has assured me that our time in England will be to the proprietors' advantage in the long run, but I see doubt and frustration in his eyes when he thinks I'm not paying attention. He so believes in the future of New Jersey. He can't bear to think of a failure on his part.

Thomas is anxious to receive correspondence from Perth Amboy to keep abreast of political news. He hasn't heard of any trouble, as yet.

I am happy to hear that your move to Staten Island went well. You sound happy to be in a Dutch community. I imagine you miss your homeland.

I send my best wishes to you and your family.

Your Friend — Janet

August 1697

My Dear Sarah,

I missed the fortnight in Yorkshire. Since I am with child again. Thomas wanted me near my doctor. You know me, I argued, but to no avail. I missed my husband, and spent my lonely hours preparing a layette.

Thomas feels that the meeting has done some good. Although he said most of the proprietors are not interested in helping the settlers, only reaping returns from their labors.

At least now we can plan our voyage back to New Jersey. London is a big city, busy with commerce and social activities. I enjoyed the diversions but miss our simpler life in Perth Amboy and will be pleased to return.

I will write again once we are home.

Yours in Friendship — Janet

October 1697
Perth Amboy, New Jersey

My dear friend, Sarah,

*While still in London, we were blessed with another
son who we named after his father. I think I will refer
to him as Tom to head off any confusion.*

*We returned to Perth Amboy a fortnight ago and are
settling back into our lives here.*

*Issy and Margaret are doing fine. Nothing has
changed for either of the poor souls. They send their
hellos to you and often talk of the fun they had
teaching you to be a lady's maid.*

*I visited Kechi. Her girls have not been found. She is
as sad as you could imagine. She keeps up with her
chores, but the light in her eyes has gone out.
Thomas has sent word to his contacts. We still hope
he will hear of a lead.*

*Thomas did his best meeting with the Proprietor's in
England, but tenants are still not paying their rents. I
hear there are riots in some areas over that.*

*Before we left for England an Englishman named
Jeremiah Basse interpreted the Navigation Act to
mean that not only could Scottish ships not dock in
East New Jersey, but Scottish men could not hold an
office of authority here either. Knowing it all to be
absurd Thomas had petitioned Parliament to make a
final ruling on the matter. On our return to Perth
Amboy we have found some gun-carrying
Englishmen threatening riots. They have even
managed to keep Governor Hamilton from his office.
Thomas hopes that the final pronouncement will
arrive soon from London.*

I hope all is well with you and your family. I would like to visit you there on Staten Island, but once again I am with child and I know Thomas will want me to stay close to home.

My best to you all,

Your friend — Janet

November 1697

Dearest Janet,

I so enjoyed your letter with all the news of Perth Amboy. I am happy that Issy and Margaret are keeping well, and, of course, I, too, continue to pray for Kechi and her family.

You know you are welcome anytime, but I agree with Thomas. You should not travel in your condition.

I am happily with child once again, too. You and I have never-ending blessings.

We are happy here on Staten Island. It is a peaceful place, I'm sorry to hear that East New Jersey is not. Our family is praying for Thomas's success with its problems.

Your Friend Always — Sarah

January 1698

Dearest Sarah,

I am sorry I have not been able to write sooner. Our little John was born without mishap and keeps me busy. When you worked for us, I'd marveled at how easily you seemed to care for your three children. I am grateful for the help I have. I am sure I could not do all of it alone. The children are all well. We managed through the winter with no more than the usual sniffles and coughs.

These days we spend our time seeking relief from the humid summer. As you must remember nightfall brings no respite.

Thankfully, word came from London clarifying the intent of the Navigation Act as Thomas had understood it. However, Basse is still in the Governorship and Thomas gives me concern. He has been traveling East New Jersey with Lewis Morris and George Willocks holding public meetings denouncing Basse's Governorship and his courts' authority. That's within the law, but after they leave town the citizens interrupt legal proceedings, attack officials, and vandalize courtrooms.

Warrants for the arrest of Thomas and his two peers were issued last month. Thomas talked himself out of a jail sentence, but the other two were imprisoned. However, before the first night was over a gang of men broke down the door of the jail and with clubs and other weapons demanded their release.

Thomas works through legal procedures to try to make changes, but he becomes frustrated waiting for results. I don't know what Thomas and his cohorts will get themselves into next.

I am glad you are not having these kinds of worries in New York. I think of you often and hope to meet again soon.
Yours in friendship — Janet

February 1699

Dear Janet,

*James and I are both shocked at the trouble Thomas
faces in his political dealings. I hope you and your
family are safe from harm even while the countryside
is in such turmoil.*

*James said he hears some talk about what's going on
there but had no idea it is in such disorder. I feel we
left in good time.*

*Our Elizabeth arrived bringing more happiness to
our family. It's different and delightful to have a girl
in our family.*

*Give our best to Thomas and wish him well in his
endeavors.*

As Always — Sarah

September 1699

Dear Sarah,

*We are so happy for you and your family. A daughter
is special. I wish I could meet her. Give her a cuddle
for me.*

*Sarah, I believe your prayers have been heard and
finally, I have some good news about East New
Jersey to share with you. The proprietors sent Basse
away and have reinstated Governor Hamilton. Scots
have been reappointed to official offices and there is
a general peace in the land. —Jane*

Oct 1699

Dear Janet,

I am so happy to hear peace prevails in East New Jersey. Thomas's hard work is seeing its fruits.

I have my first crop of sweet potatoes here on Staten Island. I wrote Kechi with the good news. Bringing the trough James built for me into our cabin saved the plants from the early frost. Having the tasty potatoes again is worth the two years of trial and error it took to discover the successful process. Kechi encouraged me through her letters, but I was not convinced I would ever triumph.

We are enjoying the last of autumn. Winter will be upon us all too soon.

Miss you —Sarah

The summer of seventeen-hundred two men arrived at the forge. Strangers dressed in what looked to James like Sunday suits. They tipped their hats and the taller one said, "Misters Van Dorn and Cousin. You are Fitchett the Master Blacksmith?"

James, not knowing which man was Van Dorn or Cousin, set down his tools, stopped pumping the bellows and wiped his hands on the towel tucked into his apron's straps that tied at his waist. He shook his head in the affirmative, "What can I do for you today?"

The same man went on, "We hear you're an honest, hardworking man and we don't want you to miss this opportunity. We're looking to settle country northwest of here, good land to cultivate and graze livestock. There's forest, plain, and meadowland near what's called The Great Swamp. We need a Master Blacksmith and you're the man we want for the job."

James brushed his hair back off his forehead. "Well, gentlemen, I haven't thought about leaving my business here. I know the difficulties you're facing, I helped settle these parts. I'm doing all right, have no need to move on."

The short stocky man spoke up, "Your family's situation will improve in Bullshead. We could offer you a seat on the town council." His words seemed to speed up as he went on, "You'd be one of the most prominent men in town. You do want what's best for your wife and children, don't you?"

"Of course, doesn't every man? But I'll need to know more about your offer before I say Yea or Nay."

James invited the two men to sit on barrel tops out of the blazing sun. He figured the way they were dressed added a few degrees to the heat of the day. The tall man answered to Cousin when the other spoke to him, which made Van Dorn the shorter, fast talking huckster. James wasn't sure he should trust him, but as James listened to the details Cousin seemed to be more considerate of James' situation.

James sat in silence for a few minutes thinking before he asked, "When do you need my answer?"

"Well, that's the thing," the tall one, Cousin, answered, "We need your answer tomorrow before we leave town. We have more tradesmen to meet in settlements between here and the Raritan River. Let's say we'll wait in the town's square until three."

"That's not much time to make a major decision."

"Maybe not, but it's all the time we have."

"And, by the way," Van Dorn quickly interjected, "if you decide to join our venture, you'll need to give us two-hundred pounds sterling tomorrow to cover your lease."

James swallowed hard. He didn't have that kind of money.

Continuing without acknowledging James' reaction Van Dorn, seemingly in a great hurry, ended the conversation, "Well, see you tomorrow by three either way. We hope you're smart enough to recognize a good deal. Good day."

Both men stood brushed the seat of their pants as if they'd been sitting in muck and walked away.

The deal did sound good to James. No longer just a tradesman, he'd be an influential town councilman. And he'd be able to provide a better life for his family. He'd be able to give Sarah finer things like his mother had had. It didn't take long for his mind to say "yes."

However, that evening when he told Sarah, she balked, "James, we don't have that kind of money. We're doing fine here. The first few years weren't easy, we struggled. But we're settled. This is our home. Who knows what we'd find in Bullshead? We need to stay put."

She seemed to pick up emotional steam as she went on, "And a swamp? The Great Swamp? Disease and pests will be rampant. Holland filled in their swamps with earth to stop the contagion, and you want to take your children to live near a swamp?"

"Sarah, I grew up near a huge marsh basin. It wasn't a killer. It was alive with hundreds of extraordinary birds. This so-called great swamp won't hurt us, I'm sure."

Lying in bed awake into the dawn James thought about Sarah's concerns, then thought back over his life. He realized he'd never made an important decision. He always followed others' direction: his parents, Ramsey his master blacksmith when he was an apprentice, Mudie whom he'd been indentured to, and now Sarah. He clenched his hand into a tight fist. A bitter taste took hold of his tongue. At supper he hadn't had an appetite. Now sleep evaded him as he tossed and turned.

He pushed the quilt toward Sarah and put his feet on the floor as slowly and quietly as he could. He didn't want to disturb her. He grabbed his clothing and boots and tiptoed out of the bedroom. He needed air to think. His stomach grumbled. He paced and finally muttered, "Bloody hell. I want to give Sarah a better life. I'm forty-two-years-old and running out of time. This is my chance . . . my last chance to succeed."

By morning he'd made up his mind. He tried to work, but with his arms weak from fatigue he could hardly hammer softened iron. Determined to take a stand and not let anyone, not even Sarah, stop him, he threw the hammer down and stomped away leaving his curious apprentice on his own.

The local money lender was pleased to accommodate James' needs. James signed a ten-year note using his blacksmith tools for collateral. Resolute, James met his new partners, handed Cousin the money and signed a contract binding him to his decision. Cousin reached his hand toward James and as they shook hands said, "James, you've made the right choice. This is the start of a new life for you and your family."

Accepting his hand in a solid shake James replied, "I believe it is. I'll get my affairs in order and move my family to Bullshead by the end of this month."

Van Dorn blurted, almost shouting, "No, James," then he took a deep breath, dabbed at his brow with a handkerchief, and spoke in a more calm, controlled manner, "We need to find more tradesmen. We'll let you know when to make your move. Until then carry on here in Cockles Town. We'll be in touch." He tucked James payment into his pocket and walked off without another word.

...

James worked sunup to sundown and often talked about his plans. However, after a few months seeing disappointment in Sarah's eyes whenever he spoke of it, he decided not to mention it until he heard from his partners. He certainly hoped he hadn't given money to a couple of thieves.

Sarah economized wherever she could. She wasn't happy about the loan with its interest, but they had to make the payments or lose James' tools. No tools surely meant destitution for her family. She determined to do whatever was needed of her. James could not fail.

She missed her friend Janet and was pleased when she finally received a letter from her.

July 1702

Dear Sarah,

It has been too long since I have written. Almost two years ago I gave birth to a wonderful little girl, Margaret. She brings smiles to everyone who sees her. And I am with child again. Now I understand what my mother once said about Ellen not being able to deny her husband. Thomas is a man in need of great comfort as he exerts his energies for our future. And in turn he gives me more love than I ever imagined possible.

Since Hamilton is back in the Governor's Office, Thomas is determined to keep him there. However, I sometimes wonder at the methods used. Lewis Morris is a rebel. This last March he convinced Hamilton to preside over court proceedings in Middletown sentencing a confessed pirate. As expected, local men disrupted the hearing, imprisoned Thomas, Hamilton, and Lewis and set the pirate free. I was frantic for those four days and nights. But Thomas returned unharmed and quite pleased that the Englishmen of Middletown, Hamilton's loudest critics, had put themselves in jeopardy of being tried for treason.

I hope you don't mind me sharing the concerns I have over my husband's adventures. You are the only one who understands my view of his efforts. I cannot discuss any of this with anyone here in Perth Amboy.

My stomach has been upset the past few mornings, I am not sure if I hope another child is growing or if I'd rather have the grippe.

Your friend — Janet

August 1702

My dear Janet,

Thank you for your letter. You know I do not mind hearing your concerns about your husband's dealings. I am not sure I would be able to handle the weight his activities put on your shoulders. And another baby. I wish you the best in your travail.

I, too, am concerned about my husband's business dealings. James signed a contract and invested in a new settlement northwest of here. It has been over a year and he's not heard from the men who offered him this opportunity. I fear they have absconded with the funds. James had to sign a ten-year note putting his tools in jeopardy as he used them for collateral. I am sure you would know I was not in agreement, but James would not hear any arguments. So, we wait and hope as we work to repay the loan. I wonder what this next year will bring for your family and mine.

Meanwhile, you and I carry on doing our best as we send love and strength to one another.

Your Friend Always — Sarah

December 1702

Dear Sarah,

I hope this letter finds you and your family well. I am often exhausted, but happy. Another healthy baby girl joined us a few weeks ago. We named her Mary.

There have been considerable changes here in New Jersey. Late last year, the Proprietors' Group surrendered the governance to the English Crown. Queen Anne united East and West New Jersey and extended the responsibilities of her cousin, Edward Hyde, better known as Lord Cornbury, Governor of New York to also preside over the whole of New Jersey.

Thomas no longer has the proprietors to speak for but continues to work toward a fair government. He hopes to stand as delegate to New Jersey's First General Assembly representing Perth Amboy. I am sure he will never give up his service to his fellow citizens. And I will stand by him as long as I live.

Mary is crying to nurse — Janet

Almost two years passed before Cousin sent a letter to James instructing him to relocate to Bullshead as soon as he was able. Relieved to know he hadn't thrown his money away, James hoped success neared. December eighteenth, 1702, a lease for a forge and cabin on fourteen acres of land transferred from Yellis Inyard to James Fitchett. The legal instrument described its size and location—eight acres of Fresh Meadow, west of the plain and between the plain and the Great Swamp.

Still paying on the loan James couldn't afford an apprentice. However, John was fifteen and strong. James taught him how to keep the fire burning and wield the sledgehammer. Fourteen-year-old Young James carried water from the settlement well to the house and the slack tub. He burnt wood making charcoal for the forge fire pit, ran errands, and delivered completed orders waiting for the time he would join the men in the forge.

Twelve-year-old Sany gathered wood for the forge and helped his mother in the kitchen garden. When he had time, he explored the woods and the swamp. Come evenings, he drew pictures of the things he'd discovered. At four-years-old Elizabeth followed her mother and played at her side.

Sarah and Janet continued to keep in touch although sporadically because both their lives had become busier every year.

April 1703

Dear Janet,

Our Effie arrived last month bringing more happiness to our family. The older children are helpful. I would not be able to keep up without them.

I've become friends with a Lenape grandmother, Nadi. She is teaching me how to use native plants for medicines. It is interesting and useful. — Sarah

May 1705

Dear Sarah,

Thank you for your note of congratulations. Euphemia is growing stronger, but I must admit I am struggling to keep up. The other children are well and learning more every day. They are quick to understand their lessons, then run out to spend time with their friends exploring and playing games as children do.

Of course, Thomas continues to demand a fair government which means he has disputes with Cornbury's cronies and again has had warrants for his arrest. But these are legal manipulations and do not come to fruition.

One humorous note, the Assembly is alarmed because Governor Cornbury opens the first session each year dressed as a woman in all the latest English finery and fashion. He says he does it because he represents a woman, Queen Anne, but the mutterings are of much different innuendoes. I'm sure you can imagine the implications in what is being said.

On that bit of naughty gossip, I will close. Your friend — Janet

December 1705

Another wee lass has blessed our home this year as well, Baby Sarah. Elizabeth thinks she is her own baby doll. And the boys continue to dote on all three of their sisters.

Sarah

January 1706

*I am so happy for your family. Baby Sarah
sounds like a delight.*

Janet

Lenape Influence

1707

James Fitchett's life had settled into a predictable routine. James never found time to sit on the town council. Instead he worked long hours to earn enough money to support his family and make loan payments as regular as possible. James marveled at how Sarah could meet family obligations and find time to befriend women from all walks of life. Janet, Kechi, and, here in Bullshead, a Lenape grandmother Sarah met while gathering purple, pink, and white azalea blossoms with Elizabeth.

Nadi sat crossed legged on the floor of the Fitchett cabin, drinking herb tea, and visiting while Sarah prepared the family's midday meal. Nadi told Sarah about her people, "Lenape first humans, other tribes still respect us. Call us 'Grandparents.'"

The native people north of Manhattan had made war against the Dutch, but the Lenape welcomed all to their shores. The old woman went on, "Before white man, we have many animals to hunt and room to grow corn, beans, and squash. Now Lenape follow the sun going down to find game to hunt and land to plant."

She continued, "What happens to my people if more white men arrive in big canoes from across many waters? I worry how Lenape to come will share the land. Already my grandsons show impatience sharing ancestral hunting grounds and obeying white-man's laws. They not live in old times but hear stories of hunting and freedom and they long for old ways."

The old woman stood and walked to the open hearth where Sarah kept embers smoldering. Hearing water bubble she picked up the kettle's lid and added more leaves she'd brought to share with Sarah. Nadi fell silent as the tea steeped. Then, looking as if she had woken from a deep sleep, she carried the kettle to Sarah and filled their cups.

Resuming her place on the floor, she continued. "I fear for our children and those to come. How they follow our ways under white man's law? How they protect themselves from unfriendly tribes? They long to enjoy all the fathers had. Nadi mean wise in Lenape tongue, but I am not wise enough. Don't know answers."

Sarah sipped her tea as she worked and listened to the old woman. She heard concern in Nadi's voice but had no answers either.

A sunny day in early May Nadi arrived carrying a small pouch in a basket. "Come, Sarah, I teach you good medicine."

Sarah grabbed a bonnet and her own basket. "Elizabeth, watch your sisters, I'll be back soon." Then following Nadi into their meadow, she smiled into the summer breeze. As far as Sarah was concerned, this parcel of land with a bounty of wildflowers was the one redeeming thing about Bullshead.

She often took the children there when afternoon chores were done, but before their evening meal. They would stand quiet and watch hawks soar through the air above their heads. They'd pick daisies, violets, and buttercups, or run with the wind to fly homemade kites. And sometimes, on special occasions just before bedtime, they'd lie on their backs searching the stars hanging in the night sky looking close enough to touch. On warm evenings, they'd chase swarms of fireflies flickering through tall grasses.

Stopping, Nadi pointed at a tall plant. Out of its hairy stalk grew delicate looking stems with green feathery leaves growing along both sides. Nadi said, "This is life medicine. English call Yarrow."

Sarah bent to look closer. Inhaling the sweet scent of its white flowers she said, "In my homeland this is called Duizendblad."

"You know this one?"

"Yes, but not for medicine. What does it do?"

"This one very good. Many ways. Chew if tooth aches, breathe steam if head hurt, drink tea when fever comes, and poultice on burns and wounds. My people use this since beginning of time."

"How do you prepare it?"

"I show you, but first must appease M*anetuwak,* the spirit who brings it to life."

Sarah watched as Nadi dug a small hole on the east side of its roots. From the pouch she carried, she pushed a pinch of native tobacco into the hole. Then she spoke directly to the plant. Sarah couldn't understand Lenape, but she felt the gratitude and respect Nadi had for the earth's bounty. Then to Sarah's surprise Nadi didn't dig the plant up, instead she walked away from it and searched for other life medicine growing near it. When the two women had filled both their baskets, they stretched toward the clear azure sky, easing the stiffness from their backs, and feeling the sun's warmth caress their faces.

Back at Sarah's cabin, Nadi instructed Sarah to tie the stems together and hang them from the rafters to dry. "In few moons, I show you how to make teas and other medicines."

After several walks to gather plants and receiving lessons taught by Nadi, Sarah learned the techniques of preparation and became practiced with many herbs. She used her knowledge and skill to help her own family and neighbors.

James saw how much Sarah appreciated the things she learned from the old woman. And Sarah showed her gratitude with small gifts—fresh fruit and jams. He also noted that John and Young James made friends with this woman's grandsons. A townsman, James lacked skills needed to survive in this new land. He approved of the friendships, happy that his wife and his sons could learn from their Lenape friends.

John and Young James were eager, adventurous boys, quick to learn.

While James and John worked together in the forge, John shared, "Pa, we're learning how to track deer. We'll be bringing one home soon."

"And just who will butcher it?" James asked.

Just than Young James showed up carrying a load of charcoal for the firepit and jumped into the conversation, "We will. We know how. Rowtag and Pajackok taught us. We'll have the venison ready for Ma to cook."

"I look forward to it, boys. Now let's get this order finished."

■■■

A few days later while the family ate the boys' fresh-caught river bass, John asked his father, "Pa did you know Rowtag means fire in Lenape? And Pajackok means thunder. Why do you think they were given those names?"

James chuckled, "The master blacksmith who I apprenticed with, Aiden Ramsay, told me in Gaelic Aiden means fire. He said he thought his parents must have known that fire would be the center of his life. Maybe your friend is destined to be a blacksmith."

"Nah, Pa," Young James answered with an all-knowing tone. "One of the other boys told me Rowtag got his name because he thinks for a long, long time. Like a long-burning ember, but then when he decides what to do, he rushes headlong, the way a wildfire rages through the forest."

Sarah entered the conversation, "Nadi did say that Lenape names are used to explain an Indian's personality. Her name means wise."

James warned his sons, "Well, I guess once your friend Rowtag makes up his mind, you better get out of his way. You don't want to get burned."

"Pa, that won't happen," assured John.

Sarah smiled, "No, that won't happen." Then she frowned as she admonished, "But you will get bellyaches if you don't eat slower."

Young James continued, "Pajackok told me his name means thunder and then the other boys laughed and said it's because he makes a lot of noise, but then doesn't do much."

James replied with laughter.

But Sarah, in a serious tone said, "That's too bad. Hopefully, he'll learn to be quiet and listen and then do worthwhile things to help others."

The family ate in silence until John changed the subject with, "Today Rowtag told us about Kishelemukong, the Lenape's Great Spirit. He said the Spirit rewards good acts and punishes clan members who choose evil. Evil acts keep Indians out of the highest heaven."

"That's interesting." James muttered as he swiped his plate with the last of the bread.

Sarah put her fork down staring at James, "Interesting? Nonsense. There is only one heaven and only God's Elect will be granted entrance."

"How do we get to be one of God's elect, Mother?" Elizabeth asked.

"Well, sweetheart, God chooses His elect before we're born. It's called predestination."

John spoke up hoping to please his mother, "I told him our Great Spirit chooses who goes to Heaven. I told him a chosen one cannot do evil, but who God doesn't want will do evil on earth and end up in Hell."

Pleased, Sarah commended her oldest son, "That's right, John."

"But then Rowtag asked if I do good because God makes me. He asked me if I could decide to do evil. When I said 'no' he said, I must be one of God's chosen because I do good."

"Yes, John," Sarah smiled, "I'm sure you are one of God's Elect."

Six-year-old Elizabeth chimed in, "Mother, am I one of God's chosen?"

"Yes, the people who are God's Elect have a strong faith and live righteous lives. They can't do evil. I'm sure everyone in our family is God's Elect."

Words spilled from Young James mouth as he interjected, "Well, my friend Sam says God allows people to choose good or evil. He says there's no such thing as predestination. That we should use our reasoning to decide what is right and wrong."

"There are heretics who teach against predestination, original sin, and infant baptism," Sarah explained. She didn't want her children to veer off the path she had known her entire life, so she ended the conversation as she stood to carry dirty plates to the wash basin, "But you don't need to worry about what you hear."

Elizabeth led her sister outside to play. Sany and John followed James to the forge, but his young namesake kept after his mother, "But don't the Elect go to church? Pa doesn't go to church. Does that mean he's evil and damned?"

Sarah faced her son. Holding his shoulders, she looked him in the eyes, "Don't be silly. Your father is a good man. Now get back to the forge to help him."

Sarah wished her prayers could save the heretics' souls, but she had been taught that God determined everyone's eternal lives before their birth. The Dutch Reformed Church saw faith in Christ as a sign of election, promise of eternal salvation. Sarah feared for Young James. His questions might be a lack of faith which told her he might be headed for eternal damnation. She shuddered to think of it and determined to intensify her prayers for her family. And, as always, she pushed fears for her husband's salvation out of her head.

...

News traveled fast, a preacher from Leiden, Holland, would be arriving in June. Sarah smiled through her chores looking forward to hearing the news from her homeland. The meeting would be held in a farmer's barn two miles away and take place on a Sunday afternoon. James agreed on Sarah's plan to take all six children with her.

Sarah prepared their best clothes and cleaned all their shoes although they'd be full of dust by the time they got there. Even the children were excited about the adventure of the walk and possibility of meeting new friends. On their way, the boys, now tall, strong young men, took turns carrying Effie and Little Sarah on their shoulders while Elizabeth gathered shiny stones and put them in her pockets.

Anticipation filled the barn as people gathered. Flaming torches lit the space. Adults shared local news and youngsters played tag. When Preacher Schoonenberg, dressed in black with a white cravat at his neck, entered, the congregation hushed, and the children scattered to sit with their parents. Sarah and her brood sat on the third bench from the front. She wanted to hear every word:

People of Staten Island,

I have come to warn America against the wickedness that began in Holland and is spreading to the rest of Europe.

There are men, men filled with evil, who are teaching against faith, against religion, against God. These ideas were born from a Frenchman, Rene Descartes, a University of Leiden student. He declares that man should reason for himself and doubt what he cannot prove.

His notions first spread to France and are now contaminating other countries. Groups are forming who have embraced these teachings, they are called atheists.

*They are heretics who threaten our people, our
beliefs, and our church.*

I am here to plead with you.

Ignore these teachings as they reach these shores.

Do not listen or discuss these ideas.

Protect your children from them.

*Keep yourselves and your families safe within
doctrines of the Reformed Church.*

Sarah's body shook as she imagined these wrongdoers freely
broadcasting their iniquity in her new world. She feared for
her children and her community. Then she remembered that
Young James' friend Sam had already spoken of this
reasoning for one's self. *It has begun already.*

Schoonenberg preached another two hours using the
Gospel of St. Matthew 24:31,

> *'And he shall send his angels with a great sound of a
> trumpet, and they shall gather together his elect from
> the four winds, from one end of heaven to the other.'*
> *Schoonenberg explained that at the last day the Lord
> will call those who He predestined before they were
> born to enter into His kingdom.*
>
> *Only the elect, chosen in God's pleasure, will enter
> into eternal exaltation. No works can save any
> person, neither faith alone.*

He must be uncomfortable, Sarah thought as she watched the
preacher. Perspiration beaded on his forehead, and his long,

curly, white wig slid sideways when his speech became animated to the extreme. The barn had no windows. No air flowed through to relieve its stuffiness. But his dedication overcame any distress his physical body may have been experiencing.

He went on,

> As Acts 2:39 says, 'For the promise is unto you and to your children, and to all that are afar off, even as many as the Lord our God shall call. Almighty God has called those saints to be saved.' Paul explained to the Ephesians in chapter 1, verse 11. 'In whom also we have obtained an inheritance, being predestinated according to the purpose of him who worketh all things after the counsel of his own will.'
> Those who have faith in Christ are the elect. There is no faith in those predestined to damnation. Let us listen to Paul's warnings to watch and stand fast in the faith . . . 'for we walk by faith not by sight' . . . So, . . . let us draw near to God with a true heart in full assurance of faith . . .

His words soothed Sarah. Her body calmed and her eyes gleamed as she imagined her family in Heaven together. Until his parting words,

> And now I leave thee with Paul's words to the Romans chapter 12, verse 3. 'For I say, through the grace given unto me, to every man that is among you, not to think of himself more highly than he ought to think, but to think soberly, according as God hath dealt to every man the measure of faith.'

This last verse stung Sarah. Fear and confusion swirled through her. Every man should think soberly. Does that mean James lacks faith? He's not often serious. Instead he finds joy in making others laugh. The scriptures say we should have joy in our marriage. Now I'm hearing that we should think soberly. How can the words of God contradict themselves? How can I know which is true?

The preacher ended with prayer in Calvin's own words. Even so, Sarah struggled to listen and add her heartfelt prayers to the congregations.

*Grant, Almighty God, that since under the guidance
of thy Son we have been united together in the body
of thy Church, which has been so often scattered and
torn asunder, O grant that we may continue in the
unity of faith, and perseveringly fight against all the
temptations of this world and never deviate from the
right course, whatever new troubles may daily arise
and though we are exposed to many deceits let us not
be seized with fear, but by thy Spirit destroy the
wickedness of our heart, and restore us to a sound
mind, that we may ever cleave to thee with a true and
sincere heart, that being fortified by thy defense, we
may continue safe even amidst all kinds of danger,
until at length thou gatherest us into that blessed rest,
which has been prepared for us in heaven by our
Lord Jesus Christ. Amen.*

As they walked back to Bullshead, they munched on the dried apples Sarah had packed and chatted about the people they'd met. Arriving home, the children greeted their father and helped Sarah prepare cold meats, cheeses, and breads. Before bed, the oldest children read from the Bible. John led the family in evening prayer. Once everyone else was in bed, Sarah washed the plates and utensils alone in the quiet. She swept crumbs from the floorboards and then slid into bed next to James. He snored in his contented sleep.

Before sleep captured her, she prayed, "Oh, God, I want myself and my family to be your Elect saved from damnation. Please, I beg you, protect my children."

···

Rowtag and Pajackok taught John and Young James how to track, hunt, fish, and defend themselves. They found Young James's use of his spyglass unnecessary, but also fascinating. They explained to the Fitchett boys that crucial skills are learned while playing native games and taught the boys how to play Tatkusk and Pahsaheman.

In Tatkusk, one boy rolls a hoop made of grape vine along the ground while the other boys take turns trying to throw an arrow or spear through it. Young James became a leader among Lenape boys who'd been playing since they could walk. His friends awarded him an eagle's feather. He proudly wore it in the band of his old felt hat, and from that point on, the Lenape called him Eagle Feather.

John explained his favorite sport, Pahsaheman, to his father. "First two tree trunks about fifteen feet long and five inches around with branches removed are set into the ground about six feet apart at each end of a long field. Teams have no set number of players, but one is made up of boys and the other girls. While the teams face one another an elder holds the Pahsahikan, an oblong deerskin ball stuffed with deer hair. When he throws it into the air all the players rush to kick it between their posts.

Boys can only kick the ball, but girls can catch it and pass it. Boys can't use physical force to get the ball away from a girl. But the girls can grab at or run into the boys. The boys have to kick the ball between their posts, but the girls can carry or throw the ball through theirs."

James smiled, "Sounds like the girls have the advantage."

"No, they're not as strong as us boys. The rules are set so girls' teams can win sometimes."

"That's kind of the boys. Is a score kept showing who wins?"

"Yes, another Elder has twelve short sticks. When a team gets the ball past their posts one of the sticks is set in that team's score row. Once all twelve sticks are used the game is over.

"Sounds like while the boys are running and kicking the ball–"

John interrupted, "Pahsahikan."

"Yes." James cleared his throat. "The boys are learning to respect the girls. I like that. You should look out for women folk."

"I know, Pa. I watch out for my sisters and the other girls, too."

Agile on his feet and quick to react, John was welcomed into any game of Pahsaheman.

···

July 1707

In the quiet of sleeping children, Sarah put her mending down, looked at James and spoke, "I received a letter from Janet today."

"Oh, how are the Gordons?" James inquired.

"The family is well, but Thomas is still having problems with Governor Cornbury."

Setting his reading aside, James asked, "What kind of trouble?"

"Janet said Thomas won the election and sits in the General Assembly representing Perth Amboy, but he and Morris have been giving public speeches questioning some of the governor's decisions. Disruptions in some court proceedings followed. Some settlers are wielding weapons and threatening violence. Rumors of riots abound. Governor Cornbury, attempting to stop Thomas by stripping his right to practice law. Janet is concerned for his reputation, but also for his safety."

"Surely, the governor wouldn't cause harm to a respected member of the Assembly just because they disagree."

"I don't know. But Janet is with child again. So, her household is keeping her busy."

James smiled as he took his wife's hand and led her to their bed. "Gordon's worries will wait for another day."

While Sany and their sisters slept at the other end of the loft John and Young James sat on their cots facing one another. The young men had grown strong. John had wide shoulders and taut muscles from heaving the sledgehammer. Young James, lanky like his father, stood taller than his brother.

Moonlight came through the loft's small window along with a welcomed cool breeze. The boys hoped that the muggy air left behind from another hot summer day would soon dissipate. Their foreheads glistened as their talk took a serious turn.

"I don't know, James, Mother might be right." John said.

"I'm sure she's wrong." Young James whispered. "There are more ideas than the Dutch church teaches. Remember that visiting preacher telling us about the Frenchman in Leiden who says we should think for ourselves. That's the same thing Sam was telling me."

"Yes . . . but Mother said we shouldn't heed that way of thinking. She said it's from the Devil."

"Ha, the Devil. Mother's holding onto old ideas."

"James, I don't understand what you want."

"I'll tell you what I want. I want to live beyond these cabin walls." Pushing his fair hair off his forehead, Young James carried on, "Rowtag and Pajackok want to leave the rule of white men. They've grown disgusted seeing their people pushed aside and tribesmen scorned while locked in stockades at the town square. They want to be treated as free men. Warriors."

"So?"

"So, they're leaving. They're going into the wilderness. And I'm going with them."

"But, James, father needs us as apprentices, and we need to learn a trade."

Young James leaned toward John and looked straight into his eyes, "You're wrong, just like Mother." He stood as if he would walk away, but then sat again and went on, "Trades aren't needed out there. We're not boys. We're men. We can think for ourselves. We can fend for ourselves, too."

"Can we?" asked John.

Without acknowledging his brother's question, Young James went on, "Rowtag and Pajackok are determined to leave and they want us to go with them. They've been hunting many years. We won't go hungry."

John looked at his brother with earnest eyes, "You're really not afraid?"

Young James fired back, "No, I'm not afraid. I want to explore the wilderness beyond the boundary of laws and fences. We're making plans and we'll be leaving soon. It's time for you to decide if you're coming with us." Turning his back on his older brother, he stretched his body the full length of his cot.

John sat stunned. Could he leave his family?

∎∎∎

Encouraged by Young James, John agreed to join in a pact with Rowtag and Pajackok. They would hunt, fish, and protect one another as they traveled outside of what white-men called "civilization."

The boys' parents would try to convince them to stay. They didn't want to hear it. Ruled by the cocky self-assurance of the young, they secretly gathered what they'd need on their own, away from settlements and cities: blankets, knives, hatchets, bows and arrows, leather water bags, dried beans, and corn.

Late one moonless summer night, feeling confident in their plans, the Fitchett boys left a note that read,

We've gone with Rowtag and Pajackok to explore the wilderness. Don't worry. We know how to take care of ourselves.

Your sons, John and Young James

The four young men met at the edge of the settlement then together walked in a northwesterly direction.

···

As the first one up each morning, James found the note on the mantel in place of the spyglass. He rushed out of the cabin looking in all directions and calling his sons' names. He couldn't see them, and they didn't answer. In panic, he ran to the closest neighbor and pounded on their door. "Please, please, help me. My boys are gone."

A man opened the door and put his hand on James shoulder, "Calm down, man, I'll gather a search party. We'll find them."

By the time men assembled, Sarah had read the note and clutching it in her hand, ran out of the cabin. "John! Young James! Where are you? Come back, please come back." Sobbing, she fell to her knees without feeling the dampness of the early morning grasses, pleading with God for her son's return. James ran to her, helped her to her feet and held her in his arms as they tried to find strength in one another.

"Where have they gone, James? What will they do? They must come back. The wilderness isn't safe."

Trying to sound reassuring James said in a wavering voice, "We'll find them. Don't worry. A search party is already being gathered. We'll find them. We have to."

■■■

Before winter had set in, Sany had learned the role of apprentice. His arms were growing thicker and his back stronger. He missed having time to draw and explore, but he was needed, and accepted his responsibilities as best as any young man could.

One unusually cold day Sany had problems keeping the fire burning in the forge's stone pit. The foot pedal that controlled the bellows kept sticking which eliminated the oxygen needed to build the fire's intensity. After the third time of relighting the charcoal, James snapped at him, "Sany, what is the matter with you? We need the fire's heat to rise or we'll never get this work done."

"Sorry, Pa, the foot—"

"Stop with the excuses. John never had problems." He picked up a lump of cold iron.

Sany's eyes filled with tears, he couldn't speak for fear of crying. He wiped his face with his sleeve.

"Well," James demanded, "what do you have to say for yourself?" Receiving no answer, he went on, "Sany, stop crying. Bloody hell, you need to be a man." He slammed the hunk of iron onto the ground.

Unable to utter a sound, Sany ran from the forge toward the forest that surrounded Bullshead.

James crumbled to his knees and held his head in his hands. He sobbed, "What have I done?" Pounding his fists onto the hard earth he asked, "Where are my sons? Will they ever return?" Moaning he went on, "I don't know what to do and now I've hurt Sany with my impatience." He pushed his forehead on the damp ground, *Please Sany, please don't leave me, too.* James wished he would wake from this excruciating dream.

Sarah shared her grief with her dearest friend.

January 1708

Dearest Janet,

I don't know how to explain what's happened to our family. We are heartbroken. Last summer John and Young James left with no warning. One morning they were gone. Leaving only a note saying, "don't worry. We know how to take care of ourselves." I pray that is true. Two Lenape friends of theirs left with them.

*As far as our families can tell the boys had prepared
by gathering supplies and food to take. Neighbors
searched but didn't find them. The fathers of the
Lenape boys attempted to track them, but evidently
their sons had hidden their trail.*

*We've not seen or heard from them since. Please
remember them in your prayers.*

*And Sany was set to start his apprenticeship with a
weaver, but now he must stay home and help James
in for forge. I had my heart set on our youngest son
taking up my father's trade. I so wanted Sany to use
his creativity and artistic skills in his work. He is
quieter than he once was and fulfills his duties
without complaint.*

I am heartsick. Your friend — Sarah

Many letters of concern and support were posted between the
two friends. And then there came a time to celebrate Thomas
Gordon's latest achievement.

March 1709

Dear Janet,

*Please congratulate Thomas for James and me on his
appointment as Chief Justice for the high court of
New Jersey. I am sure you are pleased that his career
has finally taken an upward direction now that
Governor Lovelace has replaced Cornbury.
Hopefully, Thomas' dream of a fair government for
the province will come to be. It has been a long fight
for him.*

My family is well. I miss my boys but must carry on for James and the other children. Thank you for your friendship and prayers. They give me strength.

Sarah

The Great Swamp

From 1709 to 1712, Sany and the girls grew in stature and understanding. They seemed to know when Sarah's grief over losing John and Young James took hold. Sany gave her his best drawings from his exploring and copying from the book Mudie had given him to replicate plants and animals from around the world. The girls gathered bouquets of wildflowers. Their hugs were welcome havens in her heartache.

Most days the family worked together and enjoyed what they could. In the evenings, after chores, they read adventure stories and scriptures by candlelight. Sarah and her children attended church on Sunday's and, if the day was pleasant enough, they sat on blankets and ate lunch in the meadow. James played his tin whistle while the children sang and danced. On the whole, Sarah was pleased with her life. She had no regrets about her decision to marry James.

And 1712 saw the end of the ten-year loan James had taken out twelve years previous to lease the Bullshead home and forge. There was no more worry that non-payment could claim the precious tools James had used as collateral. The money would be saved until they could support another apprentice for James. Sarah was determined to see Sany settled with a well-known weaver.

Unfortunately, sickness settled in the community in July. Steamy is the only way to describe that summer. No one could remember a hotter or more stifling season. The smell of decay was ripe in the Great Swamp. Still-air, devoid of any breeze, could not chase the swamp stench away from the settlement. The heat, humidity, and stillness made it the perfect breeding ground for mosquitoes.

Every evening the relentless insects swarmed around, threatening settlers with their deadly stings. Families kept smudge fires outside their cabins and brought children inside as soon as they heard the mosquitoes mighty buzzing.

Even with the smoke and staying inside nine-year-old Effie received a few bites. Within hours she became feverish and was lost to delirium for several days. Sarah never wanted to leave her side. She bathed the child's skin with a soft cloth dipped in cool water. She fed Effie spoonfuls of an herb tea Nadi had taught her how to make.

At thirteen, Elizabeth insisted on relieving her mother, and, for a few hours each day, Sany kept watch over seven-year-old Little Sarah while their mother slept fitfully in her overwhelming fatigue. James worked into the night, as if his effort in the forge would save his little Effie's life.

The child lay helpless and limp as the fever raged. After many days and nights of prayers, Effie's fever broke. She opened her eyes and smiled at her mother. Sarah scooped her daughter up in her arms and held her close as she whispered, "Thank God."

At least one member of every household struggled through the fever that perilous year, some ultimately carried to the community graveyard to rest in peace. When the first freeze arrived, the visiting pastor thanked the Lord for removing the plague from their settlement.

Winter brought more snowfall than usual. Mounds of snow dotted the landscape into the late spring. Most settlers survived the severe weather, but when spring finally arrived, its rains combined with the snow melt caused flooding that left standing water and mud everywhere. Farmers couldn't plow or plant their fields.

The colonists were in the habit of throwing their household garbage and wastewater into their yards letting gravity drain it down the hill and into the swamp. But this year's flood made that impossible. Uneven ground allowed pools to form filled with rotting garbage and human waste.

The neighborhood usually withstood the occasional smell of skunk spray without complaints. However, that spring the putrid stench failed to dissipate causing nausea and grumbling. The sickening odor smelled strongest along the east side of the Fitchett home.

As Sarah cleared the breakfast dishes she stopped and put her hand on James' shoulder, "James, you have to do something about the stinking water. The neighbors are complaining, and the girls and I feel sick. You and Sany go to the forge all day and don't have to deal with it."

Standing, James kissed her on the cheek and headed toward the door. With one hand on the latch he turned to face his wife, "I've been thinking—planning how to drain it. A couple of the men say I'll need to either bale the water or dig a trench toward the swamp. The land doesn't slope enough to drain this much mud and water. Some say to leave it and it'll take care of itself in time."

Sarah dropped dishes on the table with a thud, "No, James, you can't leave it. You must do something and today. Sany can help you dig a trench but have him start from the swamp. I don't want him near that filthy water."

Later that day James put Sany to work. Starting at the swamp he instructed the boy to dig uphill toward the cabin. Then James began behind the cabin where the huge pool of standing water tapered off. As he worked, one of the roaming settlement dogs arrived to investigate the situation. James shooed the dog away thinking it would smell horrendous if it got wet from the offensive water.

However, the dog insisted on having its way. It circled around the cabin and ran at full speed into the center of the reeking, muddy mess. The dog lapped the pool as if it hadn't had water in a week or more and bounced around frolicking through the odious muck.

Before James could react, water splashed his face and clothing. He spit the foul-tasting liquid from his mouth and used his sleeves to wipe it from his eyes. Shouting, "Get outa here." He waved his arms until the dog ran away.

Much later the dog returned. Having no standing water to play in, the dog rooted around the mud. James watched as the dog used its front paws to dig up whatever its nose had found. The dog then pranced around showing off the treasure it held between its jaws. A dead skunk.

Again, James chased the dog off then scooped up the skunk with his shovel and carried it into the woods. Surprised, he'd never seen a skunk with yellow eyes. He buried it deep to cover its horrific odor.

Returning to the cabin, he found Sarah blocking the doorway fists on hips, "Oh, no, you are not coming in this cabin smelling like that."

"Where do you want me to go?" James stood there with thick, wet mud covering his boots and splattered on his face and shirt.

Pointing in the general direction she answered, "To the forge. Burn what you have on—all of it. I sent Sany down with your clean clothing. He's filling a tub for your bath. Be off with you now and don't come back until the stench is gone. Supper will wait." The cabin door slammed in his face.

James shrugged. He didn't think burning everything necessary, but when Sarah made up her mind he'd best go along.

The ground dried the following week and the odor disappeared. His neighbors waved and smiled at him again. James enjoyed the feeling of accomplishment, but at the same time he couldn't explain, even to himself, his lack of energy. He chastised himself for being lazy. Sarah saw his struggle and encouraged him to rest, but he retorted curtly, "I'm not sick."

A few days later, Sarah noticed a sickly-looking stray dog wandering the neighborhood. Where its eyes should be white, they appeared yellow. She'd never seen that before, but stray dogs lived and died as wild animals. She didn't concern herself with its condition until the following morning as she sat across the breakfast table from James and saw a yellowish tint in his eyes. *Just like the dogs.* Sarah bit her bottom lip to stop from fretting as she took her plate to the wash tub.

Sarah began paying more attention to James' health and the dog's behaviors. One day the dog came by their cabin, "James, look at that dog. It looks bedeviled. Its eyes are yellow."

"That's the dog that found the skunk. The skunk had yellow eyes, too." James shook his head, "Strange, eh?"

James came down with a severe cough that kept him and Sarah awake nights. She gave him every herb tea remedy that was available, but nothing relieved his discomfort. Exhaustion and muscle weakness supplanted the fatigue James had felt the week before. He had no appetite and nausea plagued him. He couldn't work a full day. Sany, worried for his family's well-being, stepped into his father's place to keep the forge in business.

Sarah continued to watch the dog searching for signs of its recovery. But instead she saw the dog vomiting. It looked emaciated and could only stagger a short distance. In a short time, the neighbors found the dog dead and buried it in the woods.

Frightened, Sarah recognized the same symptoms in James. *But how could he have the same disease as a dog and a skunk?* She prayed for God to have mercy on their family and heal James so he could return to work.

In her plight, Sarah wrote a letter to Janet.

June 1713

Dearest Janet,

May this note find you, Thomas, and the children well.
I'm writing to ask a favor. James isn't well and can't work a full day. Sany helps, but we still can't meet all our obligations.

Elizabeth is of age to enter service and I've trained her as you and your sisters trained me. Since you know all the prominent families in Perth Amboy, would you please ask if any are seeking domestic help?

Thank you, my friend, I'll be waiting with an anxious heart for your reply.

Sincerely — Sarah

To Sarah's relief an answer arrived with good news. Janet, herself, needed help. She wrote that she'd be delighted to have

199

Elizabeth in her home. The letter included detailed arrangements that Janet had made for Elizabeth's journey.

Even with one less mouth to feed, Sany's work couldn't satisfy their needs. Sarah sold everything they could manage to live without. However, they still couldn't meet their financial obligations and feed the family. Sarah's parents passed away some years earlier and her siblings, all but Emily, had left the area. Emily and her husband Frank struggled to get by with their brood leaving Sarah no one to go to. She knew her family needed help and soon.

On the fifteenth day of June she met with an agent who represented Richmond County. She walked into the man's stuffy office, head bowed, knees weak, and stomach roiling.

The man sitting behind the imposing desk bluntly asked, "What do you want?"

Hearing a demanding tone in his voice, Sarah looked up with trepidation. The kindness she saw in his face surprised her.

He continued, "Please sit down." Then seeing her reaction, he asked in a softer manner, "Are you ill?"

Sarah almost collapsed onto the straight-backed wooden chair facing the man's desk. And stammered, "I . . . I was told . . . my family needs help." She bowed her head attempting to find the right words, but noticing her rough hands clutching her sodden handkerchief, courage failed her. She bolted toward the door. Her words matched her hurried stride. "I'm sorry. Thank you, but I must go."

Before she could escape, the man appealed to her, "Please, tell me what you need."

This time hearing compassion in his voice, Sarah returned to the chair and, mustering all her strength, explained, "My husband is ill and can't work. My son does what he can, but we can no longer support ourselves. Our neighbors have helped with what little they have but it isn't enough. I have two young daughters and I fear for their welfare."

"Take heart. We can help." The man smiled and stroked his short, well-trimmed beard. "Your minor children can stay with families that are not in distress until your husband recovers. I'm sure that arrangement would relieve your worries and give your husband time to recoup his losses."

"Having my girls leave our home would be difficult for all of us. Is there any other way?"

"No. The County officials are discussing a poorhouse, but you wouldn't want to move your family into one of those, would you?" The man's thick eyebrows lifted as if questioning her sanity. Then with a more soothing voice he added, "And, be assured, this would be temporary. Only until your husband can support your family again."

Tears welled in Sarah's eyes, "I'm so frightened and have no family nearby."

"That's why we're here, Madam, leave it to Richmond County. We take care of our own." Taking his quill in hand he got down to business, "Now, give me the details, your husband's name?"

Leaving the office Sarah didn't know if she should feel relieved or more frightened. She returned home with a heavy heart. *How can I send my sweet girls away?* "Please, God," she prayed, "forgive me."

Sarah packed the few items of clothing Effie and Little Sarah owned and included one special toy for each of them. She explained to the girls, "A nice family will care for you until Papa is well. You'll be home before you know it." She smiled to hide her fears, "I'll miss you both, but this is for the best."

Tying the ribbons Janet had sent to the ends of their braids she continued, "Be helpful to the family you stay with. Every night before you sleep look up at the moon and stars and feel my hug. I'll be looking at the moon and stars with you, holding you close in my heart."

"But Mama," Effie sniffled, "We don't want to leave you and Papa."

Little Sarah hugged her mother's leg, wiping her tears on Sarah's apron.

"It's only for a little while. You'll be back home before you know it." Sarah told the frightened children, "Remember to say your prayers. Mama will pray for you every single day, like I always do." She hugged them and had them give James a gentle hug goodbye.

A matron with a stern expression escorted by an overfed County official led Effie and Little Sarah to a horse drawn cart. The man lifted the girls into the back and helped the matron to her seat before he took his place beside her. Sarah couldn't breathe as she watched them ride away. Her little ones pleaded through their tears, "Mama, don't send us away." "Please, Mama, Please."

Sobbing Sarah remembered Kechi's grief when her daughters were taken from her. At that time Sarah had sympathy for her friend, but now she knew how full of despair Kechi must have been. She remembered praying, asking God to protect her from ever experiencing anything like that. *But they are gone.* And they're the same age as Kechi's girls when the slave catchers snatched them. Sarah, as Kechi must have, wept everyday as she went about her duties. She tried, but failed, to hide her fears from James and Sany.

Her girls were gone, and James was bedridden, unable to feed himself. Sarah spoon fed him broth and teas, but he couldn't keep them down. As James lost strength and his skin yellowed, the neighbors told her it was 'swamp fever' and assured her that some people in the area had survived it in the past. But, she thought, animals never get swamp fever, and that fact frightened her even more. Both the skunk and the dog died from whatever it was that James was suffering with. She held little hope in her heart as James lost the ability to lift his head from the pillow.

Immense guilt burdened James about leaving Cockles Town, taking his family so near the swamp and being too sick to work. He cried as he admitted, "You were right. The swamp is a killer." And begged Sarah, "Forgive me for bringing you here."

Sitting on the edge of their bed holding his hand, Sarah softly answered, "James, you've done nothing for me to forgive. The swamp hasn't killed any of us. I'm sure it was the filthy flood water that infected you. That could have happened anywhere. Please don't blame yourself. If I hadn't insisted, you get rid of it . . ."

James gasped for breath between words, "But . . . one of . . . the children . . . might have—"

Putting her fingers on James's lips Sarah pleaded, "Please save your strength so you'll be well."

But James could not be buoyed by her pleas. His hopelessness sapped any strength he had left from his body. With his last breath James sighed, "Sarah, ik hou van jou. I love you."

From the moment of James' final words, silence engulfed her. Sarah could hear no songbirds, no children playing on the green, no wind through the trees. She saw the sun in the sky but to her the world appeared a dull gray—devoid of color and sound.

She wondered what had happened to her two oldest sons. *Where are my boys? Are they alive?* Elizabeth was safe and secure in her position with the Gordons in Perth Amboy. Sany seemed determined to work his father's forge. *And my babies,* Sarah anguished. She couldn't eat or sleep for worry about Effie, and Little Sarah.

The County officials wouldn't tell her where they had been placed. "After all," they said, "you can't provide for them now that your husband is dead. Madam, you are destitute." They tried to assure her that the children were being adequately cared for and would be until they became of age to go into service. Sarah's heart broke.

Her girls would never return to her and she didn't know how to find them. She wept in desperation. *James, what am I to do now?*

Unbeknownst to Sarah, the leaders of the community, realizing the magnitude of James' illness, had found a replacement blacksmith. The leased forge and cabin would revert to the Bullshead founders. They gave her two weeks to vacate the premises.

Sany accepted an apprenticeship with a weaver in Raritan, New Jersey and Sarah wrote to her youngest sister.

June 22, 1713

My Darling Emily,

*James has passed from this life. I am alone and in
need of shelter. If Frank sees fit to take me in, I will
help with childcare and chores to offset my keep.*

Your loving sister — Sarah

Sarah spent long sleepless nights trying to make sense of her
family's losses. She remembered the different sacred beliefs
she had heard since leaving her father's home. She wondered
if God's truth was anywhere on earth or if man's imagination
had concocted wishful fancies about an afterlife.

She had never questioned her faith, but now she didn't
think her prayers were heard. She wondered if God punished
His Elect or if she had done something to upset the Great
Spirit. Her children, all baptized as infants, should be saved.
Yet John and Young James strayed from the faith. Her
beloved James had never talked about God. As far as she
knew, he never prayed, but he had been an honest man, a
loving husband, and a good father. Would God condemn such
a man for all eternity?

Sarah had many questions but could find no answers.

Sany helped Sarah pack the few possessions left as they
waited for Emily's answer. Four days before the end of the
second week Sarah received a letter extending a warm
invitation. For the first time in weeks, breathing didn't hurt as
much.

The morning of the appointed day thick, dark storm clouds
gathered. Gales of wind whipped around the corner of the

cabin. Sarah pulled her shawl tighter around her shoulders and worried aloud, "Will Frank make it through this storm?"

Sany's hand on her shoulder comforted her. She patted his hand and tried to smile, but she could only hang her head. Soon she'd be alone with only memories of James and their children. The cabin once alive with music and laughter, now only echoed her sadness. Her thoughts questioned, what will my future hold?

"He's here, Ma. Uncle Frank is here for you."

Frank drew his ox and cart to the door of the cabin and, after shaking off dust from the trip, greeted his kin. The men loaded the cart as Sarah watched making sure nothing was left behind. She watched her son closely, wondering what might come of him. She would miss him dearly.

Seemingly reading her mind, Sany hugged her tight and whispered, "Mother, thank you for all you've done for me . . . for Pa and our family. Let Aunt Emily nurse you back to health and strength. I'll write and make my way to Perth Amboy to visit as soon as I am able."

Holding his face in her hands, Sarah looked into his eyes, holding back tears, hoping her voice would not crack, "My boy, I'm proud of you. You did what you could for your Pa and the rest of us. Now it's your time. I know you'll be an excellent weaver, like my father. It is in your blood. You will create beautiful fabrics and tapestries. Write with your news. My prayers will be with you."

As they leaned their faces closer together the clouds swept apart to show a spot of blue sky for the first time in days. The sun appeared and Sarah lifted her face letting its hopeful warmth fill her aching heart.

Sany held his mother's elbow as she climbed onto the seat of Frank's cart. Then he lifted his father's duffel bag to his shoulder. His father's tin whistle stuck out of his breast pocket. He wiped tears from his cheek as he walked toward Raritan softly singing,

> *Says I, "My young lassie, I canna weel tell ye,*
> *The road and the distance I canna weel gie,*
> *But if you'll permit me to gang a wee bittie,*
> *I'll show you the road and the miles to Dundee."*

Sarah smiled through her tears, as she sang,

> *Wilt heden nu treden voor God den Heere,*
> *Hem boven al loven van herten seer,*
> *End' maken groot zijins lieven namens eere,*
> *Die daar nu onsen vijan slat ternee.*

Author's Notes

The first known record of James Fitchett is in the ship's log of the *Thomas and Benjamin*. There James is listed as a blacksmith indentured to David Mudie. According to those records, the ship sailed from Montrose Scotland on November 5, 1684, and arrived at Perth Amboy, New Jersey, in February 1685.

According to *The Settlers of Richmondtown*, one of the first to occupy land at the head of the Fresh Kil Bay was James Fitchett. A 1696 deed shows James Fitchett owner of eighty acres in Cockles Town, Staten Island. (the name was changed to Richmond Town in 1728) Another deed, this one for the Voorlezer's House, includes a note that says, "and ye sd James Fetchth children shall have free schoelling if ye sd person shall teach both English and Dutch." and is followed by his signature.

When I visited Historic Richmond Town back in the late 1980s that section of the deed had been enlarged and hung on the wall in the visitor's center.

I announced that I was a Fitchett and one of the docents grabbed a key while excitedly asking me to follow her. She led me to the Voorlezer's House and unlocked the front door. She said we could only go in a few steps because of structural concerns, but I was thrilled to stand where my ancestor had.

However, the Historic Richmond Town website altered that assumption. Since my visit the building has been studied and it is now . . . *believed that the original structure that was used by the Dutch congregation was demolished in the 1760s, and the current structure was built in the same location, likely incorporating some of the original stone foundation.* Remembering that day, visiting the town where he had lived, continues to be a highlight of my research. (for detailed information see: historicrichmondtown.org)

In 1706 James and Sarah Fitchett, with their six children, were listed on a Staten Island Census. The children are all in the age column of '16 years and younger.' Another source that year lists James' age as 45. There are no records with the six Fitchett children's birthdates so I put them where they would fit in the story.

In March 1712, James satisfied the ten-year mortgage he placed on his tools in 1700 to cover a lease in Bullshead. The last known record for James was in 1713 when his minor children were bound out by the county court because he could not support them. There is no existing record that shows whether the Fitchetts regained custody of their children.

I have no idea when or how James died. The disease I imagined for him is Leptospirosis which is the world's most common disease transmitted to people from animals. It is usually spread in the spring and autumn through contaminated water splashed into a person's mouth or eyes. The infection attacks the liver and in James' time was fatal. Today it is cured with antibiotics.

There are no records for five of James's children, but as a young man, Alexander, also known as Sany, was a weaver's apprentice in Raritan, New Jersey before he married Maria Slover of New York. They lived in various places in New York, New Jersey, and on Long Island. They had five children.

David Mudie and Thomas Gordon both lived in Montrose and sailed to New Jersey on the same voyage. The facts about them in the story are based on historical records. I do not know how either of them may have interacted in James Fitchett's life, other than, of course the fact that Mudie had taken him to America as his indentured servant.

I have no idea what Isobel and Margaret Mudie's lives were like. Their circumstances related in this book are entirely my invention.

The only event that I intentionally moved from its historical date is Ellen Gordon's death and I did that to fit the story line. Her recorded death year is 1687. Her name is sometimes recorded as Helen and her grave is the oldest identified in the state of New Jersey.

One of Thomas Gordon's cousins did run a sugar plantation in Jamaica, but Kechi's story is imaged from historical facts regarding the West African slave trade, Nigerian crops, and Igbo tribal beliefs.

J. M. Goodison

The personalities of the characters and the everyday details of their lives are from my imagination. Any errors or misrepresentations are my responsibility.

Acknowledgements

Thank you to my readers, mentors, and encouragers Karen Wills and Bonnie Smith. My appreciation goes to the entire staff of History Buff Press. And much gratitude to the book cover design collaborators Janice McCaffrey, Bonnie Smith, and Logan Lybbert. Bonnie Trush, your final review, editing, and formatting was invaluable.

The day I paid a visit to the Somerset NJ Historical Society was my lucky day. When a woman asked what surname, I was researching and I answered "Fitchett," she immediately guided me to their holdings. But best of all she gave me Dennis Cole's name and contact information. Once Dennis and I connected, we realized we were cousins and he shared his research introducing me to James Fitchett.

Fictionalized history takes a great deal of research and help from many knowledgeable people. That being said, I want to heartily thank those volunteers and employees who gave me friendly and invaluable help when I visited the Family History Library, Salt Lake City, UT, Angus County Archives, Forfar, Scotland, and Montrose Public Library, Montrose Scotland.

Heartfelt thanks to you, Aileen Taylor of the Montrose Museum. You made me feel welcome as I explored the museum's impressive collection, answered all my questions.

Then went the extra mile to ask Joan McLaren for information on David Mudie and Thomas Gordon.

A special thanks to Maxine Friedman, Chief Curator at Historical Richmond Town, Staten Island, New York for giving me permission to use the sketches of the Fitchett home/forge and the Voorlezer's House that were originally published in 1930.

The Voorlezer's Rules listed were copied from Rules of Service for the Voorlezer (Schoolmaster and Court Messenger) in the Town of Midwout, Long Island (now Brooklyn), 1666 and 1670, and is originally from Court Minutes, Flatbush Town Records, Liber D, Volumes I & II (1664-1670).

My research via Google, Wikipedia, and online library collections took me through many articles, family trees, maps, and letters. Two useful finds were John Calvin's sermons and prayers.

Information about the Lenape peoples came from two websites: www.nanicoke-lenape.info and

www. lenapelifeways.org.

I used the King James Version of the Bible (first published in 1611) for the quotes. Compared to the Geneva Bible (of 1637) which Sarah may have used, there are minor differences in Romans 12:3 and Ecclesiastes 9:9. I chose to use the King James version because it fit the needs of the story.

I also gleaned pertinent historical facts from the following books:

Atkinson, Norman Keir. *The Early History of Montrose.* Angus Council Cultural Services, Montrose, Scotland, 1997.

Beekman, George C. *Early Dutch Settlers of Monmouth County, New Jersey.* Moreay Bros, Freehold, NJ. 1915.

Nelson, William, editor. *New Jersey Colonial Records, vol 21, First Series*; Documents relating to the colonial history of the state of New Jersey, Volume xxi; calendar of records in the office of the secretary of state, 1664-1703. Archives of the State of New Jersey. Paterson NJ, 1899.

Shorto, Russell. *Descartes' Bones; A Skeletal History of the Conflict Between Faith and Reason.* Random House, 2008.

Wall, John P. and Harold E. Pickersgill. Editors. *History of Middlesex County New Jersey 1664-1920,* Lewis Historical Publishing Company, Inc., New York, 1921.

Whitehead, William A. *East Jersey Under the Proprietary Governments.* D. Appleton & Company, New York, 1856.

About the Author

A descendant of James Fitchett, and a professional genealogist, Goodison researched the Fitchett ancestral line, visited Historic Richmond Town of Staten Island, New York, where James Fitchett wrote his name into history, and traveled to Montrose, Scotland, where his story began. Both journeys became catalysts toward writing the family story interwoven with history.

You can email the author at:
jmgoodisonauthor@gmail.com

Made in the USA
Middletown, DE
06 September 2020